Rebeccah,
Read. Write. Revise. Repeat.
Talent ain't even the 1/2 of it.
Also; send me something!
[illegible]
FanExpo 2015

POSTSCRIPTS TO DARKNESS

6

Published by Ex Hubris Imprints, Ottawa, Ontario

Cover image by MANDEM

ISBN 978-0-9812731-7-4

Contents

Foreword by Sean Moreland 5
Illustration by James Greatrex

THE FICTION

Beloved by Sky by Robin Riopelle 7
Illustration by Tomasz Wieja

The Marriage of Ocean and Dust by Alexandra Seidel 12
Illustration by Rob Thompson

The Ace of Knives by Tonya Liburd 19
Illustration by Alyssa Cooper

Blood Alone Remains by Silvia Moreno-Garcia 29
Illustration by Carrion House

Eve Ago by Lisa de Nikolits 37
Illustration by Mariel Kelly

Halloumi Detox by Christine Miscione 44
Illustration by Gregory St. John

Roasted with White Truffle by Arley Sorg 56
Illustration by Carrion House

The Feast of Father Gorger by Samuel Marzioli 65
Illustration by Joel G.

Nobody Here by Bruce Meyer 71
Illustration by Alyssa Cooper

The Imaginary Friend by Gwynne Garfinkle 76
Illustration by James Greatrex

Skullduggers by Kate Heartfield 82
Illustration by Alis Kellar

The Escape by Nicole Cushing 92
Illustration by James Greatrex

Death, in Three Acts by Sara Puls 95
Illustration by M. Belvin

THE POETRY

Sandra Kasturi, introduced by Dominik Parisien 104

The Secret History of the Human Body 105
Venice Letting Go 106
Moth & Memory 107

THE CONTRIBUTORS 108

Foreword

Dear Reader,

Welcome to the fearful, fantastic feast that is the sixth volume of our serial anthology of unsettling, uncanny fiction and art!

By way of grace before you break bread, I want to draw your attention to our cover image, "The Trials of St. Sebastian (Cypress)," by transdigital mythpunk sorcerers MANDEM. St. Sebastian, most often depicted suspended from a tree and perforated with arrows, is nonetheless supposed, according to church lore, to have been healed by St. Irene following this assault, only to later (and less picturesquely, perhaps) be beaten to death with clubs. His feast day is December 20, but we like to think you can enjoy ours any day of the year.

In MANDEM's treatment of the iconic saint, the viewer's gaze is arrested as much by the mutant children who bear witness to Sebastian's punctuation as to the spectacle of his suffering, serving to remind us of the meaning of *martyr* as one who bears witness…and who, in bearing witness, is also transformed. Our hope is that these stories work a similar magic in you.

Let these untoward-looking children remind you: this meal they serve, of images and words, is a dangerous one, and as likely to devour, as to be devoured.

First, the hors d'oeuvres. We offer you two elemental openers, stories striking in lyrical intensity and evocative power. Robin Riopelle's "Beloved by Sky" and Alexandra Seidel's "The Marriage of Ocean and Dust" enter first through the eyes, portals on wild vistas, but will continue to haunt the tongue long after you turn the page.

Then, to the soup—one hot, one cold. These are two potent tales that offer very different meditations on vengeance, and the vexed relationship between violence and redemption. Tonya Liburd's frenetic "The Ace of Knives" is counterpointed by the deliberative menace of Silvia Moreno-Garcia's "Blood Alone Remains." Moreno-Garcia's story also signals the rise of another major theme of this anthology—that of urgent, all-consuming hunger.

And so on to the main courses. The desire to master hunger underlies Lisa de Nikolits's "Eve Ago," its scalpel-sharp language cutting into the ideology of weight loss to terrific effect. Christine Miscione's "Halloumi Detox," rich with mythpunk invention, beautifully complements this aromatic plate. Where, you ask with carnivorous urgency, is the meat? Next we move on to the visceral and pulptastic mythical tableaux of Arley Sorg's "Roasted with White Truffle" and Samuel Marzioli's "The Feast of Father Gorger," each of which presents a world in which ravening reigns supreme. Then, to cleanse your palate, try the melancholy magic of Bruce Meyer's poignant revision of a Homeric episode, "Nobody Here," a story whose focus on isolation and estrangement is offset by the sweet-bitter bouquet of Gwynne Garfinkle's "The Imaginary Friend."

For dessert, we leave the gravy of myth behind and turn to three toothsome delicacies. First, Kate Heartfield's gruesomely historiographic "Skullduggers" disinters ripe delight, followed by Nicole Cushing's anxious "The Escape," a terse morsel of psychological horror. Our feast concludes with Sarah Puls' incisive "Death, in Three Acts," inevitably bringing the curtain down on our little dinner spectacle.

May it leave you full…of new hungers.

Yours,
Sean Moreland & the PstD team

Beloved by Sky
by Robin Riopelle

It's not a beach plant, this one. Mountain straight up and down, deep slash, remains of the clearcut like a murder scene after forensics have taken away the body. Screef, D-ring handle in hand, plug, duct-taped fingers raw and nailess, rummage in the bag, not many left now, some Dougs, that's all, near the end of the cut block, high up almost in clouds. Screef, set down foot on the remains of an ancient branch, bend, keep balance low, quick, plug the hole with seedling. Happy little tree. Grow, fucker, grow, but she doesn't really care, not this late in the shift.

That's when she hears it.

You prepare for bears, everyone does. Especially her. Them, the girls. This time of the month. They joke about it, but it's not funny. So a bear is what she is expecting, as though bears were in the job description, which they are. She wipes sweat across her forehead, hot work, now well into summer. Bugs gone, almost end of the planting season. She knows she's loud and loud is good. She knows she is making enough noise to warn away a bear. Don't surprise them, that's a rule.

In this one way, she tries hard to be unsurprising.

She fears cougars worse, because you don't hear them coming, and you don't warn them away. They don't give you a fighting chance. They come off the treeline cold like wraiths. When she was a kid in Gold Creek, a young cougar stalked her schoolyard, eyeing kindergarteners like strips of bacon on a griddle. Will Jacobs' dad treed it, shot it dead. A good shot, a steady hand when it came to guns, if nothing else.

She's kept her line—Lorenzo's main beef with this year's batch of newbies is their inability to keep a line, and she's no newbie, her—but Brendan and Kyle and Jay haven't, or are too damn slow, or couldn't keep up with her. The Machine, they call her with awe, but she hates that name. She's no machine. But she is so good, she is alone now. Lonely at the top, she thinks.

Again. There. Where the fog swirls, maybe not fog. Cloud. Like she's already ascended to heaven. She smiles at that, not afraid of heaven.

Bears, though. Maybe not fear, but certainly respect. You can usually smell them, like a meat locker after a lengthy blackout. They roam the clearcuts, looking for small game, an unlucky rabbit, mice. You don't think about bears surviving on a diet of mice. Tasty planters like her might be a temptation, if the bear is young enough. Or sick enough.

Her hand eases to her utility belt. She has bear spray. They joked about it at the camp just last week, scaring the newbies. Her and Lauren, arms around each other, Lauren pointing to the scar on her leg she'd gotten from falling at a wading pool when she was six, saying, "Got me right there, lucky to be alive. Bear, fuckface grizzly. Young male. They're all the same. Just want to jump you."

She chimed in, catching Lauren's eye, sparkling in the well-fed night, a bottle of Jack in one hand, the other trailing a line down Lauren's back.

Highballers both, gods of the bush. Thousands upon thousands of trees growing straight and tall because of them.

Destined for the axe, sure. But not yet. Now they have time to grow, to spread their branches, to send a taproot straight down, anchor the mountain to the sky.

"Sure," she said. "Carry fuckin' bear spray if it makes you feel better. Lorenzo says it's useless and if he says so, it's a fact." Leaned in, and the newbies, Brendan and Kyle and Jay, they leaned in too and she whipped out her canister, pointed it at their faces. "Because, this close? Seriously? If your unlucky ass is this close to a fucking bear, kiss it goodbye, boys." And laughed, took the joint from Lauren, smoke curling, before passing it to Kyle like an apology.

Branches snap. Any planter would have sung out location by now. Still nothing moves in the mist. She spreads her arms, feels like she is going to sprout wings, might fly. Look bigger is the advice. Climb a tree. No trees in sight other than the babies left in her bag.

No way is she going to play dead.

Women disappear around here. Not up on the cut block, maybe, but all along the valley, hitchhiking their way out of town, or into town. Mothers and sisters and daughters. Gone. Not unloved, not un-remembered, but certainly not championed. The numbers pile up, unchallenged.

Yeah, but so? You think this is some creep, driving his car up the mountainside ready to scoop my tough ass, make me another statistic? Don't be stupid.

Still. This feels like that. Feels like she's been seen. Spotted, marked. She's been loud, meant to scare away shy carnivores, except some predators don't operate like that, do they? Some predators are there by choice, not by chance.

Heavy, it moves like it knows where to put itself, just inside the mist. She clears her throat and it comes out a growl. Like Gonzo, her dog when she was little, a reservation mutt long-legged, some combo of labrahungry-shepherd, a hollow-eyed optimist forever denied. A growl, deep in her chest, like the slow drag of match head against grit-embedded cardboard. Smell of sulfur, a sudden and specific heat.

A man steps out of the fog. Not a man. Man-no-man, she can see this clearly, recognizes the unnaturalness of him straightaway. How *wrong* he is. Her mouth is dry, despite the growling, the growling that won't stop, that can't stop. Her hair rises all along her body, a miniature forest springing to life.

The cloud on the mountain moves again, drawing across Man-no-man. At once close, and at a remove. Seen as though from the end of a telescope, real, present, yet so far away. A fever dream, maybe.

She is tired, but not exhausted. She is too young for hangovers. She knows the difference between being stoned and sober. What can be real and what can be imagined.

A man. Not a man. Real as he needs to be: slack-jawed, pale as a maggot, hair like Spanish moss. Clothes just rags, rotted with the damp, maybe, moves like a broken windmill, roll and jolt. Roll and jolt.

Between her and the end of her line, coming toward her. Coming *for* her. Smell of old death as the wind shifts, the cloud at their feet like dry ice crawling down the plant site, fingers seeking a throat.

Women disappear around here and no one looks.

Will Jacobs used to talk about what happened when you went off-rez. Used to tell her, with her white girl's red hair and her green eyes, what she couldn't understand. Dared her to believe beyond her skin. What happened when the tail of the snake was eaten by the head. Never ending circle, spiralling smaller. And smaller.

Eat your children, and you became a monster, he said that night, long ago, when he threw the empty bottle into the parking lot, smashing it into starlight. He smiled that coyote smile, hopped a ride to the ferry dock and disappeared. Swallowed whole by the city, maybe.

It grins at her, leering, lips parting like the opened belly of a gutted fish, tongue recalling the green crap you have to scoop out of a crab's body cavity before you can eat it. It takes another step, two.

She trembles, fear of course, but also anger. Anger that she is here, on her own, faced with this ravening thing. She adjusts her grip on the handle of her shovel, the best she could afford at the beginning of the season, carbon steel, feather-light, tough. She holds it by the shaft, a club. Swings it above her head. Look big, look bigger than you are.

It doesn't stop, not really, it misplaces a foot in the coiling mist, lurches to the side, recovers nicely, too nicely. Getting surer all the time. It lifts its head, catching her smell, maybe, the smell of sweat, blood and dirt, peanuts and coffee. Its head jerks back as it takes in air, takes in some essence of her, lingering on whatever palate it has.

She thinks, for a wild moment, that she might throw up. The bile rises in the back of her throat, the bitter taste of chalk and aspirin. She steps back, knowing if she falls, it will be over. That Man-no-man is capable of speed. Above her head, the shovel shakes.

Behind her, a snuff, a snort, like God finds the situation funny. Not another one, she thinks, bile still in throat, in mouth. Arm shaking. Everything shaking. She can't turn, because that would mean taking her eyes from this thing in front of her, this thing that is tasting her on the wind. But there is something behind her now, too.

The wind changes again, and branches crack, weighted with slow deliberate movement. And it is close. Whatever it is crept up behind her, closer than the swaying Man-no-man in front of her.

And there, finally, almost a relief, like she's conjured it just by memory: the smell of wet dog. Times ten. Wet dog rolled on dead salmon washed up riverside, come back to the stream of origin to spawn and die, rotting bodies food for eagle and raven. Falling back into the earth. To grow the biggest trees on the planet, skyscrapers old as Jesus.

And why she should be thankful for a bear at this moment strikes her first as funny, then as only right.

In her bag, only one left. Little Doug, a seedling. One day perhaps, beloved by sky. Now, a foot long, the size of a submarine sandwich consumed in the time it takes Lauren—oh Lauren!—to sing "Twinkle Twinkle Little Star," eyes sparkling. Match lighting somewhere inside her. Now, only a slender wand of green. But give it twenty years. Thirty. A hundred. Three.

Man-no-man. And a bear, not a dog, not Gonzo with the wagging tail. Dog and carcass and piss. That's what they smell like, bears.

She extends her free hand behind her, not daring to take eyes from the apparition at the end of her line. Thumb and forefinger holding the seedling, other fingers extended all the way. All the way to fur. Smells like dead salmon and that is good. She doesn't know if the growl comes from her, or the bear that is a literal arm's length behind her.

Man-no-man lowers its head, arms useless at its side. Not needing arms. Or hands, or anything belonging to a man that eats children. Teeth, maybe. The smell again, of human rot, of *need*, and that's what she hears, what she translates, a wave of cold sound, hissing like the intake of breath before shouting. It is so very hungry.

The cloud drifts closer. Her shovel trembles above her head, the only weapon she thinks she has, a tool to break earth to make way for trees. Most of the seedlings will die, she thinks. And those that don't will eventually become timber. All the same in the end.

She moves. A scream in her throat, heavy caulk boots not bothering to find good purchase on cloud-slicked slash, no time, only the need to see this thing gone, this once-man, this eater of child-meat.

The bear is faster. A blur of gold-tipped fur, claws like a set of German steak knives, teeth startlingly white in the swirl of heaven.

The bear is behind her, then beside her, then it is roaring past her.

The shovel slices to the side and is lost to the slash. But the claws, the claws come down, part flesh, what had been flesh, and the air bursts with confusion, wings, baby powder, fresh meat, monthly blood, debts paid. Gone in an instant.

Not her doing, but the bear's. The bear, which now rocks from side to side, finally coming to rest beside her, leaning against her for a moment, like Gonzo used to do, sends her onto her ass, sitting beside a fucking bear on the back end of a cut block in a murdered forest.

Without warning, without a goodbye, the bear shifts its weight, moves off her and into the cloud, is enveloped by mist. To her feet, before realizing she still has something in her hand, a weapon as much as the bear, more than the shovel.

The little Doug, needled pledge, tickler of heaven. The wind, as it always does, changes, moves off, reveals the sweep of shaved mountainside, pinned with tiny promises, each plugged by hand.

That night, she hands her bear spray to round-eyed Jay, whispers, "Fuck Lorenzo." Sated, she sleeps with one hand entwined in Lauren's dark hair, dreams of Will Jacobs, laughing wherever he is.

The Marriage of Ocean and Dust
by Alexandra Seidel

The searing copper is an ocean without end.

The sky was trying to drown me. There were many thoughts that came to me in the white delirium of blood loss and sheer fatigue, but that is the one that stuck, something blue among all the white. I must have spent almost two days lying there, dying in a puddle that smelled of wetness and metal. The light that came through the ghost-of-summer leaves clinging to the trees made all the earth around me look wet; so red with me, this earth of copper, this earth so coppered.

Apart from becoming a little obsessed about the sky drowning me, here's a revelation I had about why alchemists are a dying breed: they have all these strange rules, like for example *don't make a golem*, but they don't bother giving a reason. Perhaps if somebody had told me that golems are blasting strong, very nearly uncontrollable, and angry all the time, I wouldn't have lost my right arm that day.

ϛ

Burying the sea.

The golem tore it off. Grabbed it, one loam hand closing above the elbow, one below, twin vises of dirt and dust tightening, pull-twist, the sound of *me* being unmade, bright spots burning holes into my vision, but not before I see: there is the white-gray of bone, sinew strings like butchers use at the market, small pieces of flesh and skin washed away with the blood that is suddenly everywhere, a torrent of it, and the pain the pain the pain, it is inside me, the pain is me, and it *is* an ocean without end.

The golem took off, got swallowed by the woods like any wild beast, and being alive is suddenly an amazing thing, but the way life is, lying here between the leaves and pieces of me, it is really a crone's death-curse, and I want death.

I have the memory of all of it, keep it on display in the museum that is my mind, but it is a fossil of past ages, not the bones of anything that still walks this earth.

A band of Calopian traders found me, said the manticores they were taking to sell further east were going crazy with the smell of blood so close.

"So you were making a golem, a loam man?" Syph, who had been taking care of me, asked incredulously when I was well enough to talk. "You are one crazy woman then, by the suns."

"Not so crazy," I said, sitting up but still thrown off-balance by the lost chunk of meat and bone and sinew on my right side. "Just out to kill a man."

Calopians, despite their flourishing manticore trade, are essentially a peaceful people. This is why, when I was closer to life than death (closer to life: this means the skin had not quite closed over the stump, I was still pale from bleeding, and the pain like the sky, always always there), well, when I had pushed death back far enough anyway so that they could be sure they wouldn't be befallen by the bad karma of my demise, they dumped me by the side of the road with some food and water, some basic survival gear in a bag I could carry over one shoulder, and a lot of pleasantries and good wishes.

Beleros, the City of the Alchemists, was not that far away, perhaps a day's walk or so for a healthy person, for an alchemist who had lost her scripting hand (and the adjacent arm) while making a golem, it might be two or three days, I really wasn't sure.

I also wasn't sure that I would survive coming back to the city.

ς

In the theater, behind the curtain.

My mother was a gearmaker, and my father was a puppeteer. Everybody said that theirs was a strange match, something so strange that it was not made to last, but it did. In fact, they eventually combined their talents and built puppets with gears that moved them as if of their own free will. It was a marvelous thing, their *Traveling Mechanical Theater*, and they really did make a name for themselves.

Anyway, that is not really the point; the point is, my father was a storyteller and I grew up in a weaving of stories, *devils*, was even born into that woven thing. That is why I must tell of what made me make the golem as a story.

ς

Once upon a time there was a girl so mountaindew fair, even fairies were jealous of her songvoice and her nimblelimbs and her sunshine eyes (one must exaggerate, it is an essential part of telling a tale). One day the girl was playing by a blue blue river where she mixed different soils and minerals in wicked glasses and parted them again in greedy sieves. As she was spending her time so, an alchemist came along with much gravity about him as is common for these men and women of black fires and searing colors. When the alchemist saw what the girl was doing, he recognized in her immediately the makings of a fellow practitioner of his craft, and at once he said, "Girl, leave this silliness by the river and let me teach you the real secrets of this art, for only under the tutelage of a pure wise one like I will you ever outgrow the simple games of dirt and dust."

And the girl—for she hungered for knowledge like some poor wretches hunger for fairy fruit—dropped her sieves and wicked glasses and followed the eminent alchemist to the big city.

There, she was first taught the chores of alchemist apprentices of cleaning and cleansing and minding simple fires and mixing simple things into simple colors. She was quick with it all, and diligent as sphinxes are with riddles, but she desperately wanted more. However, the eminent alchemist would caution her against drowning in one's own thirst, would warn her of the proper sequence of getting her own dark alchemist's robe. "And besides, I have been at this longer than any other of my craft brothers and sisters, and I know the deepest secrets of them all; once you have studied hard enough, you as my only apprentice shall be the one to inherit all of them."

The girl did what her master told her, but she could not keep herself from growing weary when her studies seemed to be unmoving, stuck like the moons during an eclipse, caught in the sameness of a life spent as a fairy slave.

It was upon a night of triplet blood moons that a second alchemist crossed her path. There was a masquerade ball in the big city, and since masquerade balls call up all sorts of strangeness and enchantments and creatures of questionable pedigree alike, the alchemist's apprentice did not think it amiss to attend. She made herself a mask with all the dull colors she knew, and she found herself some skirts like bells in the eminent alchemist's dusty attic, and when night fell with the rising of each moon, she snuck out of the house and entered the ball like a sylph riding the Western Wind.

"These colors! Who has made your mask?" said the second alchemist, forgoing both pleasantries and introduction, and thankfully also a dance, for it is not part of an alchemist's apprentice's studies to learn how to dance.

"I made them," said the girl behind the mask, and one thing did lead to another, and the girl-apprentice never went back to the eminent alchemist's house.

Instead, the second alchemist shared all his knowledge with her, shared all his secrets with her like they weren't even secrets, like he had dined on poets' blood and could not stop himself from talking.

The sands were flowing though, and soon what had to happen happened: the eminent alchemist found out where his apprentice had vanished to, and he felt himself betrayed, quite bitterly betrayed. An alchemist betrayed—especially one who has secrets—is not a bottled djinn, he is a chimera riled, a sleeping giant woken, a snakehead maiden roused from her mirrorsleep. The eminent alchemist was like chimera, giant, and snakemaiden combined and driven into a killing frenzy, and of killing there was plenty and then some. The details are just brightest scarlet and so hot they are blisters on my tongue, but the essence of it is, the second alchemist was killed like the hero of a tragedy, bodies of the other players stacked behind him, but with his last shardsharp breath, he pushed the girl right off the last page of the bloody tale, so the heavy, wineblack curtain would never take her head.

ç

And so I made the bloody golem, to get back at the old quicksilver heart who killed *my* alchemist.

ç

Succor the copper from the lips of the ocean.

Walking back to the City on stumbling feet, I counted two problems: old Finyarr and the golem.

I did not know what to do about either to be perfectly honest, I had lost all my skill with my arm, for alchemy is something that needs hands. And the golem, the golem was unstoppable for a cripple like me, and it knew me too, like only a made thing can know its maker.

I was really fairy-bitten, as they say.

ς

Swallowing salt, or, drinking the ocean.

Instead of going on to Beleros, I turned like the wind turned, walked back, but not away. I somehow managed to find that clearing again where I had made the golem, although I felt the tendrils of fever-fog drifting in to hide the way. There must have been something broken inside me already that overcame the fever-fog, because that broken thing wanted to return to the place where it had been snapped into pieces; or perhaps it was just a dumb roll of the fortune god's dice, or the sky overhead that kept trying to pull me in and drown me.

I saw the pond-puddle of copperred off to my left, and scattered all around the bits of loam and dust and dirt, the bits of soil I'd scattered while I made the body-shape.

The fever-fog makes it hard to remember, but this part is clear in my museum of recollection: the idea came to me somewhat like lightning, like the revelation that alchemists have doomed themselves to die.

ς

Learning to write the hand of true wisdom.

True wisdom is a phrase alchemists use as a metaphor for scripting. As if forming an arm from copperearth wasn't hard enough (you do not want to know about the smell; I do not want to remember the smell), I had to teach myself scripting with my left. I used a stick, and the earth was patient with my efforts although I felt my body growing impatient—or rather, impotent; I did the best I could in the time my body would give me, and as a museum piece this time of learning is at least a giant's thimble, but it cannot really have been that long.

I was not sure where best to put the script, but decided in the end that it had to be my tongue. I used some woad that grew nearby and a piece of stick sharpened as best I could.

It is said that a true alchemist can script in pitch black darkness, but try to script your own tongue first, I dare you, now there's a real challenge, lump of muscle swelling evermore in your mouth and blood, some of it you swallow but most of it just runs down your chin and neck and stains your shirt and goes on further to your breasts until it pools in your lap and makes you wonder if the pain of birthing could be worse. And you still cannot stop for the script must be finished.

I was lucky I guess, with the pain of the stump distracting me.

ς

Reel in dirt and dust, loam for bones.

The dressing had long since gone a blackish shade of brown because I had been out here in the wilderness much longer than was strictly sensible, and because I just wasn't able to change it on my own, even though the traders had given me enough clean bandages to do so.

I pulled it off, and there was the stump. There was still a little blood where Syph had sewed the flaps of skin together, also yellow-sick puss. The blood

would help to bind the copperearth arm to the stump, but I had to pull the thread out of the skin. That hurt less than the work on my tongue had done, but when I suddenly felt the bone beneath my fingers, I felt sickness taking me like a wave. I kept going though, then lay down again in that puddle, moved the stump to the copperearth arm, and felt more than saw the binding.

ς

The earth will eat.

Inside me, there was something that went suddenly quiet and small and silent and cold, but there was also something bigger that woke, and it felt like that bigger thing broke free, shattered a door that had kept it locked away all my life, before.

When it was done, I was just…different, part golem, part…

I have no word for what I was before the binding and the script, but anyway, that's gone, nothing more than an insignificant museum piece.

And another museum piece that I was staring at with fresh eyes: what had the Calopians done with my lost arm? Where were those bones that had been a part of me for so long? Would they have fed it to their manticores?

ς

The canyon that eats the sea, she keeps the water deep down in her belly.

The single-mindedness was good. I would have called myself single-minded before, but there were always so many things that I was thinking about, so many options I was considering and weighing against each other that this is hardly true. I still had all these other thoughts, but with my tongue still raw and the alchemy coursing through every drop of all the humors in me, it was so simple to just make them background props, like those little cardboard toys my parents used in their puppet shows. Inconsequential, meaningless. Something that you don't mind losing or throwing away.

I really just wanted to kill Finyarr.

The copperearth arm is a strong thing, it is fast, ruthless, knows no sickness, and some of its traits pump through the rest of my body because my blood is also in the earth. I was no longer a cripple stranded in the woods who had to crawl back home, I was running there on two strong feet and with a heart unyielding as diamond.

ϛ

In the theater, the curtain is parted, dust rustles to the stage.

I would like for it to be a story worth the telling, even though my voice is siltier than it was. I would like for it to be a play, a hero coming home wearing vengeance like a cloak.

But the truth is simple as farmer's bread. I just smashed his door in. It gave like a cardboard prop, and Finyarr came running into the hallway on account of all the ruckus, the white of his eyes making his robe seem all the blacker.

"You!" he shouted before my first punch broke a couple ribs. He couldn't talk more afterwards, so Finyarr's last word was "you," which, personally, I think is rather anticlimactic. Anyway, I don't really remember all of it, but there really wasn't much left of him when I left, pieces of bone on the floor and some of it sticking to the walls, wet and mushy pieces everywhere. I had his blood all over me, but that didn't really register, and I was lucky that it was night and that there wasn't anyone out on the streets, or they'd have pointed and shouted "Monster!" or something.

Anyway, I left the pieces of him there. I also left Beleros, pretty sure I'd never return.

The woods to the east were somewhat welcoming, at least that's what I thought when I had room in my head to think again, when the taste of Finyarr's blood on my tongue subsided and my mind became less clouded with its flavor.

I wanted to rest, make plans, but I couldn't, there was too much flaring heat inside, there still is, so I just kept on walking.

Around the crack of dawn—the hour when the souls of the dead leave the dreams of the living—I met him, the golem. I cannot say why he is a he, I certainly did not add these details to his loambody, but it feels right somehow. The eyes I gave him—polished things from the bottom of a blue blue river—were so dark in the damp light, but I knew he knew me. He lifted his hand—his right—and touched it to the pendant he had made for himself, a crude thing, but the best a golem's untrained hands can do. For a second I thought he'd come at me again, but he just passed me by, did not even look back over his shoulder.

And I was standing there, not turning to look after him either, but *devils*, I was wondering how he had known how to work my bones into a pendant, however crude it was, and also, were these really all the bones I'd lost? What had he done with the others, the shattered one for instance of which a part is even now bound with the copperearth arm? And also, what had he done with all the flesh, who wouldn't wonder that.

I was standing there wondering, and while I wondered my tongue began to itch, and it was itching for a flavor like a cloud in my mind.

It hit me then. My golem knew me, knew me in the primal ways that are all a golem has for knowing: knew me not for who I was, but for what I had become, knew me for his mother-sister, earth-of-his-earth, the only thing he owned in the entire world, the only thing who like himself was full of fire.

And even though we went our separate ways that morning, that is just the way I know him too, my earth and dust, my bone and flesh brother-son who walks like I, unresting. *Burning.*

ς

If he must be made, he must be made of his own likeness.

And so, you see, this is personal, very, although I have never met you, my brother alchemist, last of a breed to be extinct by morning. Perhaps if you think of it as a play, you will understand that I had to find an ending for it, perhaps if you think of yourself as a player, you will not mind the red velvet so much.

Thanks for purchasing!
— Tonya Liburd

The Ace of Knives
by Tonya Liburd

The Ace of Knives remembers the first time she saw the card.

The Ace of Swords, the signifier of change.

Back then she imagined the Ace of Swords to be a sign of hope. Hope that her life would improve. Instead it had been an indicator of the change she was about to undergo, that her time was coming.

It was after that reading that she became the Ace of Knives.

The Ace of Knives has an audience.

She wishes they would leave. They should. After all, they'd already been dodging her knifeplay with the other blades she'd made; the sharp things would enter their personal space, their eyes would widen in alarm. Now they were staring at the most recent blade she was honing without any tools, a former can of soup, logo still visible on the handle. A child could be heard asking, "Mommy, how does she do that?" "Hush," says the mother.

She starts singing a song the blades suggested to her.

He blocks out the sun, this black man, that's what makes the Ace of Knives look up, sitting on the grass in College Park.

She stops singing at the top of her voice. Other patrons in the park cheer, probably because she stopped the noise. The Ace of Knives ignores them.

He has a camera around his neck. "So it *is* you." He looks like he is about to cry. "She have she voice, you know…" he says softly to himself, looking away hastily, wiping at one eye, touching the camera around his neck.

The Ace of Knives lands him one of her best cutting stares.

"An' I can tell yuh off yuh meds…and yuh ain't bathe." He looks pained. "Oh god, little gyal. Oh god."

This man was beginning to anger her.

"Wa' da FUCK you want?" she asks him.

"Yuh don't remember me at-all." He looks like he is about to cry again.

"I ask you a *question*." She sits up. What the hell is his problem?

"Nah-nah, nah. Yuh parents deserve better than this. This ain't right." He flips open a cell phone and talks into it. Sunlight flashes off rings on his fingers as he walks away.

What did he just say?

"Who the *fuck* do you think you are, talking about my parents? WHO THE FUCK DO YOU THINK YOU ARE? That's right! You better walk away!" She throws after him every acid-tinged invective she knows, Canadian and West Indian.

He sits in the distance, at a chair opposite the waterfall, looking back at her occasionally.

She grips the grass in angry fists, blades coming away, green staining her fingers. "What you doin' sitting 'dere, looking at me? Come standing in my face, talking about my parents… WHO DA FUCK DO YOU THINK YOU ARE?"

He's off the phone now. Still occasionally looking her way.

"Okay now, come along." Officers walk over to her.

"YOU! YOU CALL THEM! I'll make you pay for this!"

The officers sigh, faces hardening into fists. They charge forward, grabbing arms, legs. Like zombies all clustered around her, all reaching, pulling, and she fights, squirms, can't get away.

She keeps right on flinging insults, obscenities, anything she can think of, at the standing figure of the man staring after her in the distance, camera around his neck, while the officers cart her off.

ς

The Ace of Knives has finally been pushed over the edge.

The magic in her blood demands that she kill something; the man who'd gotten her committed had just volunteered for the position.

But first, she must get out of the hospital.

From her bed she hears footsteps approach the door of her darkened room. Probably nurses at this hour.

"Poor girl," says a female voice from the doorway behind her, the tone high, light. "Every time she comes in she's always so…sick."

"Is she talking?" asks another female voice, the tone leisurely, low.

"No."

One of them tut-tuts in sympathy.

"Do you have any idea how the blinds were cut that way?" asks the leisurely toned one.

"No," High-tone says. "She was checked for sharps when she was admitted, then again earlier today…" Her voice fades off.

"Hm."

Under the covers, the Ace of Knives' ringed fingers search for reassurance. They touch the thin blade, embedded in her copper-toned flesh. It is still enchanted by her touch.

Leisure-tone speaks up again.

"She was *furious* when they brought her in, eh…"

"*Really*?" A chinking of bracelets. "She's normally so…quiet."

"Mmm…" The note drawn out in sympathy. They finally shuffle away.

The Ace of Knives lets out a soft, exasperated breath.

Her nose ring, a former circlet pendant, flashes in the corner of her eye; it reflects the annoying light from the antiseptic hallway. Her eyes move to the window, the slashed blinds now giving an unrestricted view of the stars outside.

Wide, free outdoors.

She closes her eyes against her racing mind. The hours will pass slowly, in this sterile, confining space. Everything, everything in her screams *no more medication.* But she has to be a good little patient and take the bitter pills, or they won't let her leave.

But medication will mess with the Ace of Knives, and with her magic, she is certain of it.

And she needs her magic right now.

ς

The Ace of Knives is annoyed. Again.

Earlier, in a misguided attempt at conversation near the glassy office, the Ace of Knives endured yet another indignity. She indulged someone's need to talk: the nurse with the high-toned voice from last night. High-tone promptly assumed that the Ace of Knives' family were blue-collar, working as labourers or something unskilled. The Ace of Knives smiled thinly, and said without a touch of emotion, "They're white-collar."

The voice of an older male inpatient, seated in the hospital's common area, snaps her back to the present. "What are you?" he asks.

With her head's layer of downy black-brown hair, the Ace of Knives was blessed with the good fortune of being hard to place, thanks to being dougla: having both black and East Indian parents. This fact garnered its own share of annoyances, as evidenced today.

"I'm sorry?" she almost snaps. "*What am I?*" Not a good question to be asking at this time, for more than one reason.

"I can't tell," the man says in a barely softer tone, continuing, oblivious. "Where're you from?"

"I'm Canadian," she snaps this time, and moves away from the eating table to clearly indicate the conversation is over.

As she walks away, high-tone nurse says, "Good. You're talking, and not just with me. That's faster than usual."

The Ace of Knives says nothing to this woman. She locates a spot on the plastic of the blue-grey couch and flops down, focusing on the television.

Involuntarily, a ringed finger, laced with emotion and magic, finds the thin blade under her skin, tracing its path.

The older gentleman also flops down at the opposite end of her couch, slight scent of body odour, slight amount of greying facial hair, slight potbelly, slightly balding, pale skin, pale gown like the one she wears, the type worn by those who either wanted convenience, or didn't have privileges yet to wear anything else, as was her case.

She hopes there shall not be a third annoyance today.

ς

A fellow patient wants to do a Tarot reading for the Ace of Knives.

"Let me do you," Rochelle says, wrapped in her concoction of pink robes: a pale gown for a shirt, fuchsia bedroom slippers, headwrap and an assortment of bracelets. She sits across from her at one of the smaller tables in the ward's common area.

"All right."

A pale, delicate hand places the Ace of Swords, her wrist jingling with the motion.

Again, this card. Change was coming.

She needed to get out of here; yet there'd be no way she can hide not taking her medication. For now. Medication which brought about its own changes. A dulling of the mind. A sluggishness of the senses, the spirit. This the Ace of Knives cannot abide.

For the Ace of Knives fears all drugs, be they "self-medicating"—like her parents took—or prescribed. She will live with her magic unaltered on the outside, for good or for ill. And no over-the-hill person in a park, who couldn't mind his own business, rubbing salt in the wound that was her waking life so far, would get away with his interfering ministrations.

Not anymore.

She stares at Rochelle's display of cards, and again at the key card that mattered, absently fingering her nose ring.

So, change was once again afoot?

Then, soon. Perhaps soon she would have to start hurting others. The magic in her blood had been demanding it, after all.

If she couldn't have another's blood, then for now, her own blood would have to do.

ς

The Ace of Knives knows pain.

The marks on her body are milestones of pains past.

In the damp heat of the running shower, she asks herself, *Where to put a new one?*

Here? A knee injury, from a cousin; killing any dreams of a promising track career. No.

Scratch marks, scars, looking like an animal had a go at her.

A burn mark, like a cigarette, or maybe a cigar. She breathes in the clean scent of soap in the stall to push that memory away. No.

The only mark not self-inflicted was from the fight that ended her parents' lives, that one night.

Then, everything changed: that one day, that one time. That one period of pain. Thoughts to fingers, words to mouth, tears to eyes.

Blood to skin, to air, to blade.

They say that the manifestation of one's magic is determined by the crucial events and influences—internal and external—surrounding one's "special time" which happened during puberty. Signs and markers can help point out specifically when one's special time will manifest, but the Ace of Knives was alone. No supports, no people trained to detect.

In other cultures, one might undergo a rite of passage, perhaps by spending time alone in the woods until a wolf spirit or similar animal's essence made known its affinity. The only thing she ever felt, however, was constant emotional pain, and the desire to relieve it.

That one day, that one time. That one period of pain.

And she'd found that she could sharpen metal, hone blades, enchant them with words, either deliberate or spawned from the heat of passion.

Only afterward did she realize why she was able to score her skin with a once-blunt object.

She cannot quite control her magic yet. But when the emotions are there, when she is laid bare, and the time is right, magic happens.

Banging from the next stall. Voices from outside; was her time in here nearly up?

She chooses a spot now along the edge of her chin.

The red of her blood washes away in the shower stream, swirling down the drain.

This is her answer to the magic's demands, for now.

ς

When you're young, lived a life full of pain, it's easy to think you can go all the while alone.

Better alone than in bad company, right?

But then you get older, and you realize you can't really do it all alone.

Not only that, you get sick of the isolation. You figure there has to be a better way.

The man responsible for putting the Ace of Knives in the hospital probably thinks this. It is probably why he tried to help.

But the Ace of Knives does not consider what he did to be helpful at all. More like the act of an over-the-hill busybody. Someone messing with her life. Adding to her pain. Interfering. Besides, her magic was still crying out for blood; it might as well be his.

ς

The Ace of Knives likes to cut flowers. If not fresh, out of slivers of wood.

A flower each left on their graves. A flower for anyone else's grave she feels drawn to. Through rain or shine, fog or clear, she's only comfortable there; outside. She feels safer under the gaze of the stars, a hard wooden green park bench beneath her.

Despite having an apartment, she still feels safer outside, even now. Her parents were murdered, inside.

Run for your life. Through a window, onto hard asphalt, never mind the pain, run, run. Blend in outside where they can't find you.

Outside she stayed until the police brought her to the terrifying confines of the inside, kicking and screaming. Harsh hands. Pale faces, grimacing to hold onto her. Her fear; *the murderers will get me, they'll find me*. The fresh, painful memories, like a wound: the insistent banging on their apartment's white door, the elevated voices, the breaking bead curtain, her mother's screams, the blood. Hoping and praying they wouldn't find her, hiding. The scuffle, the cut, the fleeing.

Here, she knows the names of virtually every person without a home in her area, some of them well. She'd sit on the pavement, or sleep in College Park, watching the night above, soothed by the rush and spray of the waterfalls. She'd only go home to wash up, then go back outside to be free again.

But she knew something wasn't right inside her. She'd heard horror stories from her parents. Witnessed their passing. And everyone who lived outside agreed: *you didn't trust those who controlled everything on the inside, with their ways to maim, control and hurt. At least you knew what you were getting living outside.*

Life is hard. Life is unfair. But you get harder.

If only the Ace of Knives could become so. After her parents, after her family, after everything, she was more like beaten and abused fruit.

Maybe now, with this magic to aid her, she had a chance. Could become hard as…a knife. And as sharp.

ς

The Ace of Knives is home, shaving her head in her seldom-used, overheated apartment.

It had been short before, but she felt it was time for a change. Others had been leaving their mark upon her life, right? Well, this man was the last one. Others did what they pleased, why shouldn't she? Perhaps she should have struck back sooner.

"Where the hell is he at?" she asks her magic, wiping away beads of sweat. The Ace of Knives eyes a map of the city pinned to a wall. She throws a sharpened blade; her magic guides it and the point slices deep into the wall, showing her his location.

She has found the person she needs to kill.

She grabs her shoes, shoving them on and lacing them up too tightly.

This nosy older gentleman will get a taste of comeuppance. He's not the one who has to go to the hospital. He's not the one who has to endure notions of superiority, mocking laughter, physical abuse by officers who enjoy being more rough than they have to be. He's not the one who has to deal with hospital staff who don't care, misdiagnosing you, locking you up, drugging you, suggesting solutions to problems you don't have while not helping with the pain you do.

Well, vengeance is what happens when persons with misguided notions set things in motion, then put what they started out of mind.

She fingers her nose ring.

Plus, he sealed his fate by invoking the memory of her parents as some sort of pretense.

The Ace of Knives storms out the door.

ς

The Ace of Knives is going to kill him. She is certain of this.

She is in the hallway before his door. Unpainted, varnished wood, a brass knocker. Nothing else besides the obligatory peephole.

Ringed fingers, rings that her parents wore, grip a knife. *Your interference ends here*, she vows.

Memories of humiliation flood the Ace of Knives' mind; of being isolated, people not wanting, not caring, to understand her.

A stroke of the finger; the surface of the knife is rough. Filings clump to her skin.

Memories of cops slamming her against the wall, laughing at her discomfort, of curls of the lip and the holding up of noses.

A stroke of her finger; the surface of the knife becomes smooth.

Memories come of her parents' faces, of their warnings, of her being beaten by subsequent guardians, of doctors who blame instead of help.

Her enchanted finger strokes the surface of the knife again. It becomes finer. Razor sharp.

Her hand bangs on the door. No one answers the Ace of Knives.

"Where is he?" she hisses under her breath. A trilling from the surface of the knife on her fingertip. "Is he inside?" she asks it. It warms to her touch. She inserts it into the lock. "Open the door." The knife moves quickly, surely, the lock clicks. A well-placed punch and the door flies open, slamming against the inner wall, rattling on its hinges.

And he is *there*. Seated upon a fancy rattan chair. Waiting. Holding a painting of her circlet with a heart on it, back when it was a pendant, the pendant she now sports as a nose ring. A painting from *home*.

"What are you doing with that?" she demands.

"I painted it," he informs her, his voice a deep baritone. "For your parents. For you."

The Ace of Knives doesn't know what to make of this. The fire within her sputters, endangered by a strong wind.

Various pictures cover his walls. At a small shrine sharpened objects, candles. A large photo of him with her as a baby, smiling beside her parents.

"*Who are you?*"

"My name is Clive. I'm related to you. I'm an illegitimate child in the family, so people act like I don't exist. But I do."

Clive. She remembered the name being spoken around the house. Clive, who disappeared, left her parents wondering. Clive, who was important to them. Clive, who was missed. *Uncle Clive*.

He places the painting he holds next to the diminutive shrine, then looks back to her. "It's been a few years since your parents died. A hard few years. But you're still young."

This makes the Ace of Knives freeze. *You're still young*. Many a person abused their power or authority over her waving around that oppressive notion. Her finger stretches to the knife. What other misguided notions does he run on?

"And when I say you young, I don' mean it as a bad 'ting. I mean it in the sense that there's still time."

This man will not dissuade her so easily. "Time for *what*?"

He makes an expansive gesture with his free hands. Hands with rings similar to the ones she herself wears. "Time to heal. To grow. Time to still do what you *really* want to do with your life. You really want to be doing this?" He was speaking now like a Canadian, with deliberate, gentle tones, to add space, defuse the tension of the situation.

The Ace of Knives pauses. She had *thought* she wanted to kill this man. But…maybe what she really wants is to stop running. To stop being afraid. To stop hurting. To not be so alone…

Ringed fingers in the act of clenching give away her inner turmoil.

He shifts in his rattan chair, the wicker crackling. "Trust can be…the world to a child. The witnessing of the death of one's parents is a terrible, terrible thing. It can destroy the fabric of everything you know. You couldn't completely trust your parents…could you?" he asks.

It was true. But the Ace of Knives will say nothing.

"They got…high around you, kinda scared you, didn't they? You knew things weren't quite right even then, when you didn't have the whole picture."

But they were all she had.

"Look around. Please don't see what you think you want to see. I hope that you see someone who wanted to be sure that you were stable enough for them

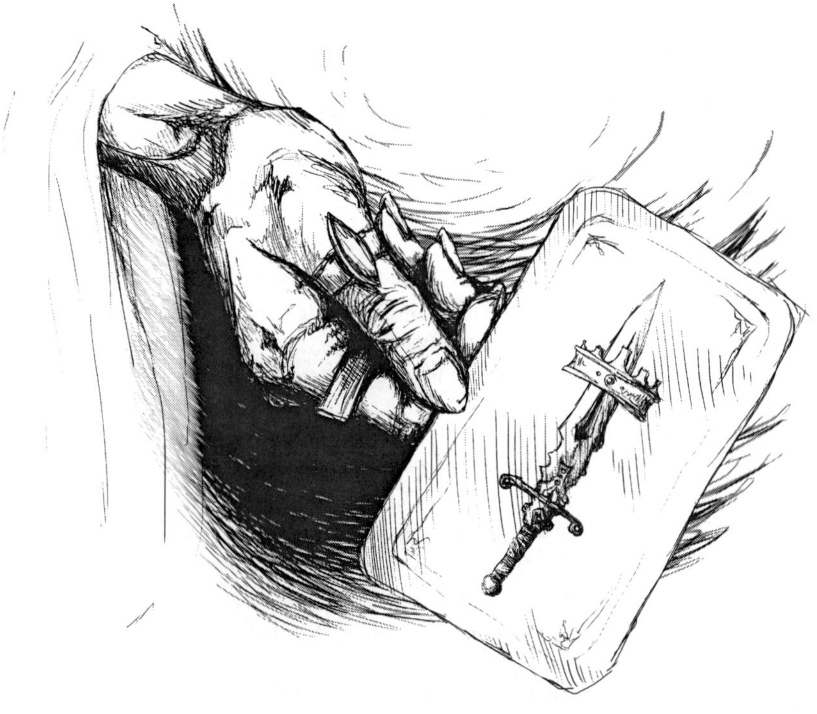

to guide you, someone who had to make sure they had their own shit straight before they took on the task of caretaking someone else's child, someone who is here now, here for you, someone who will always be here, whose place, arms, and heart will always be open for you. Unconditionally. And I promise, if I fail in any of these things I am promising to you, you can do what you came here to do to me."

One breath.

Two.

Three breaths the Ace of Knives takes.

She says two words: "Keep talking."

Warm, gentle patois: "Yuh want to take a seat, Keisha?" He indicates another rattan chair.

Would she be making any signs of conceding? No, the Ace of Knives will not. She will, however, take a few deliberate steps inside. Closer to him. Hands clasped behind her back.

He nods. "You've been traumatized. Deeply. It will take years to overcome this kind of damage, my dear. It may always still be with you, but with the right help, it won't cripple you. And you will need help, of various sorts. To complicate matters, you've inherited mental illness—it runs in the family. And you cannot do this alone. There will always be people in the world who can hurt you. But your magic won't be affected by medications; I know this from experience with other people. It can be adjusted. It will aid you in thinking clearly. You can tell that already, can't you? Even from that small amount of time you spent taking them at the hospital. And with clarity, you can direct your magic in ways to help it thrive."

He fingered the pendant he wore that matched her nose ring. "I can also guide you. I can be there to protect you in times of pain, and... Well, for your illness...there will be ups and downs. You will have to learn to prepare for them, and ride them so you don't get smashed into the rocks. But it will take time. And, again...I promise, that if you accept my help, I will be there."

He smiled gently at her. "How I doin' so far?" he asked, slipping into patois again.

The Ace of Knives has to make a decision. Before answering, she takes her hands from behind her back, and puts the knife away. She closes the door, comes round the rattan chair and places it before him, before she sits down.

"Keep talking."

ϛ

The Ace of Knives is crafting wooden flowers on the sidewalk. Nearby are woodcarvings of various patterns and shapes. People are standing nearby, slowing down to admire the work, watching. Purchasing.

She is putting her skills at cutting to good use; something...positive. Attainable. Useful. But she still likes to be outside. One thing at a time.

It seems like the Ace of Knives has found a friend. Not only that, an ally. A support, even. It would appear that the cards foretold an improvement to her circumstances this time around. She never seems to guess those cards right. That ability was obviously not her forte. But something else was.

What else could she do now?

Perhaps, look into the history and uses of her namesake.

Perhaps it was not such a bad thing that she did not have to kill.

Perhaps now she could actually live up to her name, and truly become an Ace of Knives.

Blood Alone Remains

by Silvia Moreno-Garcia

"The resemblance is uncanny," she said.

"That's funny. I've always thought I look more like my grandmother."

"No, you look exactly like Charles Gregory."

The hair was different, but every other detail matched the old black and white pictures she had seen: the arrogant eyes, the high cheekbones, the aristocratic tilt of the head. As if to reinforce the similarities the man took out a cigarette and lit it, leaning back in the plush chair.

Jazz music played. From a turntable, not a digital device. Trumpets. Evocative, moody, the slight scratches on the record bringing the composition to life.

The man smiled, a practiced expression that lacked mirth and skirted boredom.

"If you say so," he said.

She twisted the ring upon her finger, a plain silver band. *Daniel 7-7*, it read on the inside. Her grandfather's gift to her. He'd insisted on it. He'd been a stern man, rigorous. She could still recall his voice as he read out loud a passage from the Bible before breakfast. At nights, another passage. The monotony of their existence was broken by the black and white movies. She remembered in particular a scene when the bad guy shoots the hero and there's no blood. She'd asked Grandfather why there wasn't blood and he said they wouldn't have shown it back then. The Hays Code.

"It's very nice of you to take the time to talk to me," she said, grabbing her knapsack and searching inside it. "Do you mind if I tape this?"

"No, not at all. Do you need me to lower the volume of the music?"

"It should be fine. Thanks for asking."

She placed the recorder on the coffee table sitting between them.

"This is a very nice place. A bit out of the way."

"It was my grandfather's home. He liked the privacy. There's no one for miles around."

The house was old, large, clearly the abode of a wealthy man. Above the fireplace sat a large movie poster from the 1950s exclaiming in large, block letters ENTRAPPED. Charles Gregory did not appear on the poster. Instead, the focus of the artist had been on a woman in a long cocktail dress. *Don't be seduced*, warned the tagline.

"His first movie," she said, pointing at the poster. "1949."

"He got third billing."

"That's not bad, is it? Have you seen all of your grandfather's movies, Alan? Can I call you Alan?"

The man nodded. He seemed bored, more concerned with his cigarette than her, taking a long drag and opening his mouth, smoke curling out in the dim light of the living room. The house was rather dark and cold, though the man did not seem bothered by the temperature. He was not wearing a sweater. The fireplace was off even though it was the end of October. She had kept her jacket on when she walked in.

"Sure. I've seen three of them. They're not easily available. My grandfather wasn't a famous man. He made minor movies. They've been forgotten. I was surprised when I got your phone call. I didn't think anyone remembered him."

"Well, *my* grandfather knew Charles Gregory."

"Oh?" the man said.

"Well, he kind of knew him. He saw all his pictures. His sister was a big fan of Gregory. She had a collection of Gregory memorabilia: photos, magazines where we appeared, that sort of thing. I inherited it and I guess it was only natural I'd have an interest in him, you know."

"Would you like a drink? Brandy?"

His eyes were very attractive, mesmerizing. But if you looked carefully you noticed an odd…absence. It was hard to describe.

She glanced down at her hands, touching the ring.

"Maybe later. After we've talked about Mr. Gregory."

"It's nice to know someone remembers his work and very nice of you to drive out here."

"It was a good drive. And it's not like I had much to do, you know? Writing gigs are hard to come by these days, but I'm hoping this piece will be my big break."

"Well, I'm glad to help. It's not like Granddad was famous."

"He would have been a big star. Only five movies, though. Why did he quit when he was on his way to stardom?"

"I wouldn't say he was on his way to anywhere."

"But he was. He'd made *Unholy*, his first lead role. Can I take a closer look at that?"

She pointed to a poster hanging on the other side of the room. *The Thirteenth Floor*, it said. It was painted in stark greens and reds. A man pointed a gun at the viewer, a beautiful woman stood behind him. And behind the woman was Charles Gregory, cigarette in hand. Second billing.

"Evangeline Jones," she said.

She turned to look at Alan, who was tapping his cigarette against the ashtray, the slightest frown upon his face.

"What?"

"That's Evangeline Jones. She was also an up-and-coming actress. Oh, come on, your grandfather must have told you about her. They were engaged."

"I recall something, vaguely."

"Well, I suppose she didn't leave as big an impression as Louise Locke, but he must have mentioned her, no?"

Alan looked at her with a very serious face. He no longer seemed bored or distracted. His attention was entirely focused on his guest. She felt she was being dissected, every single item of her quickly classified, from her jacket to her boots.

“Oh, come on, you do know who Louise Locke was, don’t you?” she said, playfully.

“No.”

“Louise Locke moved to Hollywood in ’54. Very beautiful, kind of mysterious. Nobody really knew where she came from. Some said she was the ex-mistress of a French count, others that she’d worked as a maid in Chicago. She went to Los Angeles with a boyfriend producer, Blake Dermott, but she lost interest in him. She took up with Charles Gregory. He was already engaged to Evangeline, though.”

“I imagine he broke it off.”

He had a very smooth voice laced with the texture of velvet and fog. And his eyes, as he leaned forward, clasping his hands together, had a fascinating shine to them.

She focused on the facts, as she knew them. They were part of her by rote and she could summon them easily, the details anchoring her.

“He didn’t have to. Evangeline died in 1956, shortly after Charles shot *Unholy*. He left California with Louise Locke just days after her funeral, I’m surprised he didn’t tell you this story. It was a bit scandalous.”

She walked across the room to stand in front of a headshot of Charles Gregory in profile.

“That’s from *Unholy*. His last publicity shot.”

“You really are a big fan of my grandfather, aren’t you?”

“Of course. I know everything about him. His natural hair colour was blond though he dyed it black for the films. He had a little scar on his chest from an accident he had when he was 12. And his mistress’s name was not really Louise Locke, it was Iryna Lysenko.”

Alan stood up and moved to her side, his eyes fixed on the black and white photograph. And though he did nothing but stare at the image, there was something enticing about him. As though he were willing her to stretch out a hand and touch him.

She reached into her bag and took out a camera, snapping a shot of Alan, the flash going off and bathing him with light. He stepped back, irritated.

“I’m sorry, I should have asked if I could take your picture,” she said apologetically. “In fact, I should have asked you to sign the waiver before I took the picture. Sorry. I’m just so happy to be here. It’s my first big assignment. Are you okay?”

He touched the bridge of his nose, clenching his teeth.

“I’m fine. Iryna—where did you hear that name?”

“I can’t take credit for it. My grandfather was the one who made the connection. She had so many aliases! You know what’s the funny thing? People said she was a vampire.”

“A vampire,” Alan said flatly.

“Not one of those romantic vampires. Eastern European folklore has all these horrible stories about vampires. There is a story about a man named Jure Grando who died in 1656 but came back from the grave to terrorize his village until he was decapitated years later. Nowadays there's a vampire themed bar in the town where this happened. It's decorated with garlic wreaths and crosses. Can you believe it? I suppose that's the way it goes. Monsters become entertainment, they become sexy. But there wasn't anything entertaining about the original stories. They called them a str…strata? Streta? God, I can't say."

"Strigoi."

"Yes," she said, smiling.

She sat down again, waving distractedly in the direction of the turntable.

"Charles Gregory was a big jazz aficionado, too."

"I know. I have his records," he said, mimicking her and sitting in front of her.

He bent forward to put out his cigarette. He was very tall, very thin, reminded her of a praying mantis. Good looking, though. Most people must have noticed the good looks rather than the odd boniness of his limbs, the way he sat. Like an animal waiting to pounce.

"So what do you think?"

"About?"

"The vampire story."

"I'm surprised anyone would have been telling vampire stories in the 1950s."

"There's always been all kinds of odd tales going around Hollywood. Did you know, for example, that James Dean's car is supposed to be cursed? Or that one of the Munchkins in *The Wizard of Oz* committed suicide while filming the movie? Never mind a decapitated Jayne Mansfield."

"And Elvis is alive and living in Berlin. Such silliness."

"I think the stories are kind of cool. Take Evangeline Jones. Not only was she killed, she was savagely murdered. Her whole body cut into little pieces. The coroner said at first they couldn't even tell the remains were human. She was butchered."

"I thought we were going to talk about Charles Gregory."

"We are," she said with a prim smile. "I'll take that drink you offered me now."

He smiled back at her. He knew how to smile. It was a well-practised expression, warm, kind, thoroughly attractive. She pictured him in front of the mirror, perfecting it. Just the right amount of charm. Nothing to put anyone off.

He walked towards the liquor cabinet.

"How did he die?"

"Old age," he replied.

"Five years ago, am I right?"

"Yes."

"In this house?"

"The hospital."

"You know, it's funny, I couldn't find his death certificate. I looked."

"Not close enough."

"No, very closely. Just like I looked very closely at Iryna's trail," she continued, "the girl from nowhere who vanished one fine day. Only she didn't really come from nowhere because if you look back carefully enough you see a very definite trail. It stretches back to 1845."

The needle skipped just as Alan turned around with the two glasses of brandy. He did not seem surprised when he saw her pointing a gun at him. His face was impassive. A block of granite.

"What do you think you are doing?" he asked.

"Shooting you," she said, and pulled the trigger.

He did not scream when the bullet pierced his shoulder. He barely moved, his reaction seemingly delayed until he loosened his grip on the glasses. They shattered against the floor.

"Silver bullets blessed by a priest. I'll empty five into your gut if you try anything."

"You crazy bitch," he muttered, taking a step back, resting a hand against the mantel of the fireplace.

"I'm not crazy, Charlie."

"What did you say?"

"Charlie."

"What—"

"Charlie. Charles Gregory. You thought you were so smart, only you weren't. You made mistakes. Starting with the murder of Evangeline Jones."

"Damn it, I'm hurt! I'm bleeding!"

"I can't leave now, Charles, we have unfinished business."

"What are you going on about?!"

He rubbed a hand against his shoulder and looked at the blood on his fingers, then up at her.

"Evangeline Jones. Murdered, cut into little pieces."

"And what? *I* did it? I wasn't born then!"

"Yes, you did it. Evangeline had a brother and that brother saw you. He saw what you did and he hid and he was terrified. But he grew up, became my grandfather, taught me about your kind."

"Holy shit, do you realize what you are saying? That I'm some sort of… monster? A vampire? And that I killed my girlfriend for no good reason?!"

"Initiation."

"What?"

"Iryna turned you, but there was a price. An initiation ritual. You had to show you were ready for it. You murdered Evangeline to get admitted into the vampire club."

He shuffled back a bit.

"Don't move. You don't want two more bullets in that chest of yours, do you?"

"This is not *Dracula*! What are you, some psychotic Goth chick?"

"2,300 people are reported missing every day in the United States."

"And what, they are killed by vampires? Vampires who made noir movies and lived in Hollywood five decades ago?"

"Unbutton your shirt."

"What?"

"Unbutton it or I am going to shoot your dick off and vampire or not, it's going to hurt a whole lot."

He obeyed, fingers steady as he worked the buttons, exposing his chest. She smiled.

"Charles Gregory's scar. Still want to say you are not him?"

"Coincidence. Everyone has scars. Look, I'll give you money, I won't call the police, no one ever has to know—"

"Give me her location."

"What?"

"Tell me where Iryna is."

He sagged against the wall, taking a deep breath.

"I don't know where she is."

"If you tell me I won't shoot you."

"Someone must have heard the shot. Someone must have phoned the cops. You should get out of here now."

"Someone? There's no one for miles around!" she said with a cheery smile.

She took a step forward. His hand was splayed against the wall, shoulders hunched. He was looking at the floor and gritting his teeth.

"I know what you thought. All those little questions you asked on the phone, about me. The assignment. Was I on staff? Just a freelancer? Would it disrupt whatever plans I had for Mother's Day? Oh, mother dead? And father too. Pity, that. You were trying to figure out if you might be able to dispose of me without anybody caring. And you thought you could. Wrong."

"You need help. You need a doctor."

"Where is Iryna? What's she up to these days?"

"I have no idea what you are going on about."

"Tell me and I won't shoot you. I know you are in pain. That's the problem with these blessed silver bullets! They are a damn pain in the neck, pun intended. You are going to lose consciousness very soon. In, oh…five more minutes, I think? Although we could speed it up with another bullet. And when you are fast asleep I'm going to shoot you up with a nice garlic extract and cut your head off, how does that sound for fun?"

He said nothing.

"Silver bullet to the dick it is."

He looked up at her and his face was a mask of savagery, distended with rage. And there was no longer anything remotely attractive about him, nothing human. He jumped towards her, his hands wrapped around her neck, cold as ice and hard as iron, his mouth open so very wide, like a shark's maw and his teeth seemed black, blacker than black.

She raised her hand, pressed her ring against his cheek.

Silver, blessed.

He loosened his grip on her.

She shot him twice and shoved him back. He fell flat on his back, twisting upon the floor. There was a lot of blood, pooling around him. Very red. Not like in

the movies he'd starred in where such details were omitted for the audience's sake.

"You know what's the problem with your kind?" she said, rummaging in her knapsack. "You get really cocky and really lazy after a few decades. Once upon a time you would have been ready for the vampire killers. But not anymore."

His eyes were wide open, his lips curling, trying to mutter something.

"After this I saw in the night visions," she muttered. "And behold a fourth beast, dreadful and terrible, and strong exceedingly."

He kept opening his mouth, opening and closing it.

She found the knife and glanced back at him.

"And it had great iron teeth: it devoured and brake in pieces, and stamped the residue with the feet of it."

His eyes were red. Red as the blood fanning around his body.

She made the sign of the cross.

He let out a vicious roar, like metal striking metal, and stretched out an arm towards her.

"And it was diverse from all the beasts that were before it; and it had ten horns."

She lowered the knife.

Eve Ago

by Lisa de Nikolits

I once knew a woman so fat she wore her body as a gown.

Her appetites were killing her; she was eating herself to death. The question posed by many was not why she was killing herself but rather why she had chosen to do it so publicly, and in so naked a way.

I was a member of the hungry pack that fed on her lifeblood; my lens ever-poised to take that money-making shot and capture that tell-all moment. We chatted among ourselves while we waited, and we tried to figure out the whys, and sure, intense were the speculations and some of us even asked, but no one ever knew.

Clear to all though, were her unchecked appetites, in full view, on display.

Her Willendorf Venus body had become a curiosity, a freakshow, conceptual art. She paraded herself in public, aided by three attendants who escorted her wherever she wanted to go.

At first, there was an outcry, she's naked for God's sake! But then, no, she's *art*.

Breathing mightily, she attended soirees, parties, galas, red carpet events. She was hauled out of limos and helped to glittering occasions, her buttocks no longer sexual but artistic and curious, her breasts pendulous, blamelessly innocent of provocative allure. Her hanging stomach hid any hint of her sex.

She won crowds of supporters and at the urging of the rich and the famous, she indulged them, allowing them a shared moment in the spotlight, to feed her. It seemed like everybody wanted the privilege of handing her a delicacy; giving blessed the giver, like touching the Buddha's belly.

The ultimate socio-memorabilia was to be photographed with her, one hand permitted to cup an overflowing breast. A signed autograph was given, and a picture on her official website followed.

But who was she, I wondered, my camera heavy around my neck, the taste in my mouth rancid and stale from cold old coffee and waiting. Who was this hidden woman? Who lived inside that mammoth and careful construction of accumulated flesh and blood? What thoughts privately circled the small quiet streets of her mind? What choices had she made, why had she decided to exit so publicly and yet so silently?

And, while I watched for days, months, I grew none the wiser.

She revealed nothing of her origins; when introduced she'd smile, remain silent and allow herself to be touched with the inscrutable grace of a supermodel.

She was the topic of blogs and talk radio, newspapers, magazines and TV, and all acknowledged with wonder that the fattest woman in the northwestern world was never seen gorging on buckets of ice cream or gnawing on chicken wings or blarney nachos covered in thick yellow cheese.

No, not one for cream puffs, Oreo Cakesters or takeout food courts was she. She was all quality all the way, five-star cuisine. She nibbled and snacked 24-7 but only on high-end gourmet delights.

Tasters brought her new concoctions; a never-ending parade of exotic delicacies and her tiny, prettily accepting hands fluttered, pale and manicured. Never was her bare chest sullied by a drip of liquid or a morsel of food. Nor did she lean unattractively or gluttonously towards food; it was as if she were absent from her ever-constant eating. And yet eat she did; continuously, steadily, delicately. Almost, unremarkably.

I tried to make eye contact with her, I tried to get as close to her as I could but I was sure she never saw me, or any of us.

She came by the name *Eve Ago*, her clearly fictitious existence supported with perfectly forged documents, her showy life planned with precision and when probed to confess, she would only smile. Her face was anonymous, sunk too deep for individuality or defining characteristics and what she had looked like before she ballooned no one could say. Her hair was bouffant platinum candy, Marilyn-styled by a hairdresser, and we could not guess her age.

She was assisted by a secretary, a plain, older woman, dried out, skinny, businesslike and stern. She took care of Eve's social calendar from the edge of a televised heart-shaped white-satin bed and she advised Eve of the events of the day.

The secretary would advise us too, she'd come to the door and read out an itinerary in one continuous sentence and we'd have to be quick to get it all down.

Eve never commented, she went as directed while three boys clucked and fussed around her. These milk eunuchs bathed her lovingly, laundered her sheets with scents of sugar vanilla and fanned gentle breezes through a bedchamber kept fragrant with floating notes of coconut and cocoa bean (as noted on her website).

Eve stood tall, nearly six feet. She wore no makeup, save the barest of face powder to eliminate unsightly shine. She was also trailed by a young makeup artist with purple hair and multiple piercings who would dab and stroke. The girl was an outside recruit, not part of the boys and the secretary who were close-knit and close-mouthed. The girl was the one who told me that Eve never spoke even when she was alone with the boys. I tell you, it cost me, just getting that useless piece of information. I wanted to know who Eve really was.

And I wondered, conceptual art crap aside, what was it that had led to Eve's popularity? Was it the allure of watching a slow, naked suicide? Had reality TV finally lost its appeal to be replaced by a real-life freakshow?

Eve was offered jewellery from Bulgari and Cartier. Fragrances from Dior, Versace and de la Renta. She waved them all away. She declined a range of her own body products. Jenny Craig offered to help her slim. Plus-sized couture, designed only for her, was rejected.

She accepted nothing except food. And that she accepted, without reservation.

For a while, before she became too large to move, she dined out. Maître d's seated her in the windows of their front rooms where she ate alone. Her attendants, on hand behind her, flitted in now and then to adjust, and darted out. They never ate or drank. The secretary and makeup artist sat together, with the three boys off to the side. None of the entourage ever spoke to outsiders except for the secretary in her tidy tweed suit. And the makeup girl, when I had enough money, but she could never tell me anything juicy. She did tell me this, that there was one proviso to the restaurant dining: Eve had to be seated in her own chair, which would precede her arrival. The chair was a gold-leafed, red-velvet throne and Eve sat in the centre, a large pearl in a scarlet jewel case.

That cost me a hundred dollars, that nugget about the chair. As if I hadn't already figured that out for myself along with the rest of the world.

Eve grew larger by the day. Doctors fought over ethical concerns. Magazines argued the message, advertisers bid their wares, psychiatrists had a field day. Eve graced the cover of *Time*, *Vogue*, *Harper's Bazaar* and a pack of us rats followed in her wake. She was bigger than any fly-by-night teenage celebrity or movie star. Literally bigger. Right, pathetic joke, but believe me, you'd be tired too, following the Michelin poster girl eighteen hours a day.

And the more that was seen of her, the less was known.

People stepped forward, claiming they knew her from her past, they said, but they were soon proven liars. Some even claimed to be offspring. Husbands and so-called lovers stepped into the light only to be discredited.

And still, Eve never spoke. And soon, she grew too heavy to move from her bed. She went inside the house one day and that was it, she never came out. Not great for my particular employ; for us *celebrity photographers* this was the end of the road. But I couldn't help myself, I hung around. I just had to. So instead of photographing Eve, I photographed the endless baskets of beribboned food delivered to her house from every corner of the globe. I didn't do too badly off that either, I got to know the couriers so I had the scoop and you've got no idea how many people wanted those shots like asap, man.

And Eve, well, her breathing grew laboured and her days became numbered. How did I know? It was on TV. The secretary woman invited CNN to sit in Eve's bedchamber, hour upon hour. It was not enough to have a silent, installed camera that whirred invisibly; the secretary demanded lights, action, trendy anchor hosts.

The phenom caught on; watching this fat woman die became an international obsession. From Australia to London, Iceland to Japan, the world watched Eve eat and die.

Social moralists condemned the fixation and ordered her banned. Free-speech proponents shouted nay and the feeding frenzy continued.

I stood outside and wondered how Eve was, during all of this. I wondered if she was in pain or discomfort. I felt that if only I could get to her, I could help her. I knew I'd be the one able to make that breakthrough, I just knew it. I could save her, I was the one who understood her.

But all access denied was denied, there were locks on the windows and grilles on the doors. There was no way in. There was a time each day when cameras were shut off and outsiders ousted. Then the acolytes would bathe Eve, massage her and change her satin bedding. Her bedchamber was aired and freshened, flowers whipped into vases, cushions patted and plumped.

During their breaks, I tried to pump info from the anchor hosts who had been inside but they were squirrelling away their nuts for their own shows and tell-all memoirs.

And then recess over, it was back to the endless eating and watching.

Eve began to sleep during the day and she woke late at night to eat. She lost her regular audience but gained insomniacs, shift workers, mothers with colicky babies.

The distressed, the disturbed, the lonely, they all watched her; there was a kinship. They felt they knew her intimately, in ways no one else did. As did we, us dwindling hangers on. I increased my vigil, not going home at all, camping in my truck instead where I had a TV installed.

And then one day, a change occurred.

The secretary woman ordered Eve's favourite foods from her most cherished chef and made the announcement that this would be the last meal Eve would share with the world.

I had no idea what I'd do once this was over, the mere thought frightened me. I could not imagine my life without Eve. I hung out on the lawn while caterers rushed around preparing the last supper.

That final night came and Eve, propped in bed, feasted laboriously. The mood was somber. In front of their televisions, many dined with her, having prepared the identical meal. It was an international occasion, a solidarity farewell.

Supper over, Eve's boys lovingly removed the gold-leafed rose-patterned plates. Eve looked directly into the camera and with unblinking pale eyes, cut the connection.

And that was all we ever saw of Eve. We, her followers, were inconsolable. The lonely returned to being alone.

Eve vanished inexplicably that same night after the last supper. The TV cameras had been told to leave quickly after the connection was severed and even I was sent away. I drove away with my eye on the empty street in my review mirror; it was ghostly, ominous and dead.

I went home, had a shower and slept for two days.

And what happened after we all left, no one knows. The house was shut and boarded. The acolytes, the secretary, they too disappeared, never to be seen or heard from again. They refused to emerge, even for the promise of obscene sums of money from hundreds of relentless magazines.

People presumed Eve must have died that last night. But what had become of her body? Too large to walk anymore, too large to get out of a door, they would surely have had to knock down a wall and had firemen at the ready. There had been much speculation over Eve's demise; when it would happen, how it would be handled. Many anticipated with grisly delight all the indignities Eve would suffer with her removal and burial, and even I was curious, curious and ready with my long lens and my power flash.

But that was all for naught. We were banished and Eve disappeared quietly that last night, even then denying us the morbid pleasure of our suburban ideas of closure.

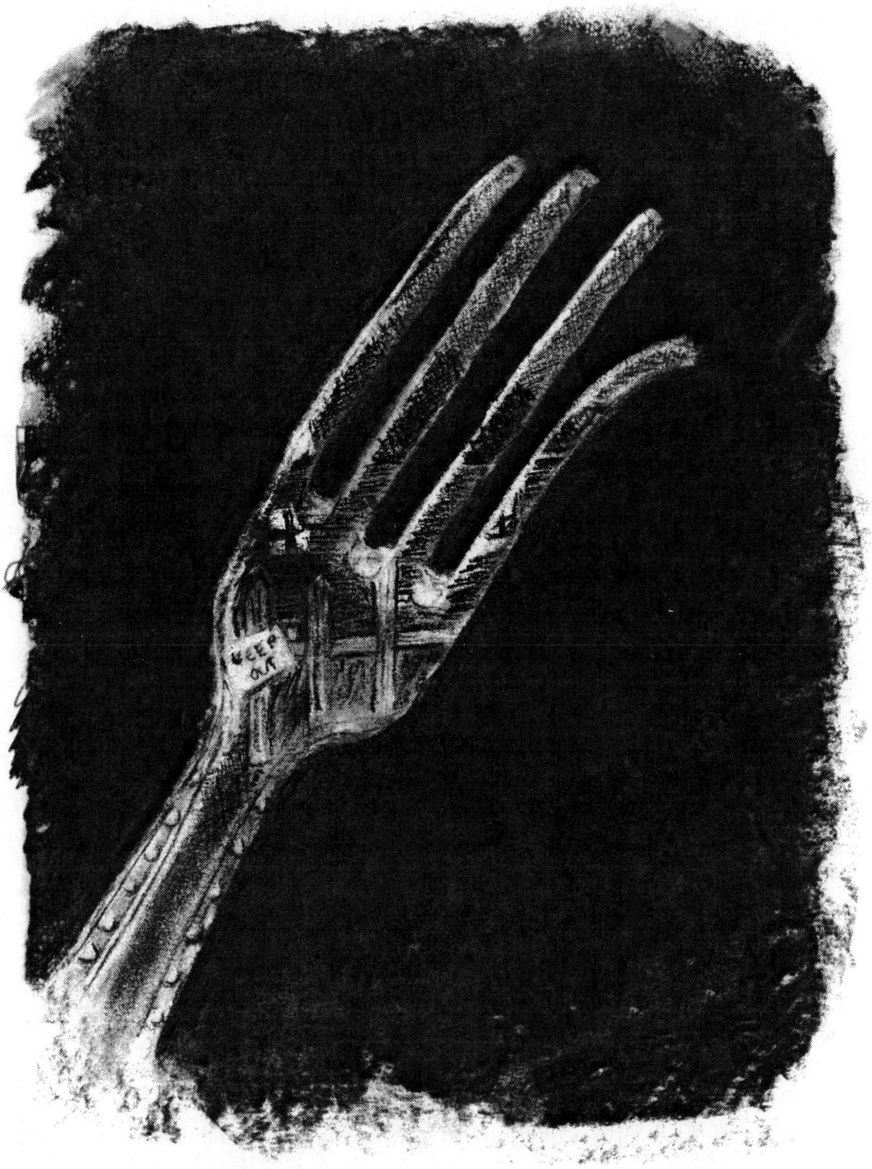

I went back to following B-list celebrities while around me others still clamoured for detail, unwilling to let go, and the scavenge hunt continued.

These days not much can remain secret forever, and a few facts finally emerged, blinking their way into the tabloid light.

Relentless research into the backgrounds of the boy assistants and bitter secretary eventually revealed that the strange clan was a family: three brothers, one sister. Pale, featureless and plain, they hailed from a tiny, unmemorable town. School photographs showed small, thin adolescents. At school events they were sticklike, underfed, anti-social.

Reporters talked to everyone and received noncommittal replies that shed dim light. As far as they knew, the reluctant townsfolk admitted, the parents died when the children were very young but the kids stayed together because no one in town cared enough to bother with them and besides, they didn't seem to need no help no how.

The children grew up in a rotting sagging wet ivy-covered house of green wood and in the photographs, they looked as though they had never seen a day of sun in their lives. They stuck close, never talked, never socialized, but they studied hard at school and made passing grades.

But who, and where, was Eve in all of this?

I read that one of the neighbours mumbled something about a baby having come from some nonsense between the sister and her brothers but, when pressed, she fell silent and would not be drawn out.

Another neighbour, a gnarled old lady twisted with arthritis, said that she had seen dead animals scattered in the yard when she went to visit. She had, for a period of time, tried to befriend the children and lend a maternal hand but they would have none of it. She had wondered then if the gutted destroyed animals had been purposely arranged in an attempt to discourage her visits but when she peered through the kitchen window, she swore she saw similar raw remains on the kitchen table. Shortly thereafter she decided to leave the children to their own devices.

She said that apart from these things, which, she added, she probably should not have mentioned anyways, the children were just fine; clean, their clothing well-pressed, they were always on time for school. Two of the boys were twins, she said, identical except that the one boy had green eyes, the other blue. Pale as milk they were, she said, even back then.

Of the eldest, the girl, the secretary, not much was known, oh except, added a crone who could have been man or woman, that the girl had been the one to discover the body of her mother in the icebox in the basement. The mother had been chopped up and stored limb by limb. A large woman, she had filled the large box entirely.

The story went that the children had lived for years alongside the silent padlocked refrigerator in the basement until one day the eldest girl, overcome by curiosity, got the local locksmith to visit the house. Twelve she was, at the time.

Appalled by the tragedy, the townsfolk rushed to the aid of the children who were interested in none of the affectations of support. They said thank you quite nicely to all offers of assistance but they would take care of themselves.

The townsfolk reckoned that the father had disappeared about the same time as the mother—it had been assumed by all that they'd driven off together, tired of the responsibility, tired of life's chores. Others believed they had walked into the forest never to return, choosing to live off the land, which had been their way.

More wild speculation followed in the wake of these revelations; Eve was an incest baby, fathered by her brothers, mothered by her sister. Fed to obesity, she was plumped and primed on the world's finest delicacies, and then she, in turn, was feasted upon by her starved brothers and sister who had been denied by the world for so long. A sacrificial lamb was Eve, groomed to feed the revenge of her disturbed siblings.

But nothing was proven and the remaining four could never be found.

The world soon forgot Eve and moved onto the next roadside attraction.

In-crowds dined out on stories of other misfits while I, still obsessed for no good reason, made my way to her house many years later and broke in. The house that I had watched from the outside for so long. Unable to let go, I needed to try to find a clue, anything, that could give me a hint as to what had really happened.

But the house was a ruin, and all I found was the graffiti of bored children who had come before me leaving paint cans and scattered beer bottles. There was no furniture, the ceiling had long since caved in and the wallpaper crawled down the grey walls in damp paisley floral strips covered with green mould.

I found a rickety old dresser in the kitchen, I pried the drawers open with difficulty and found a single fork, ornamental and curlicued, black with age, the tines bent. I picked it up and wondered if it had been used to feed Eve. It was long and elegant, an antique no doubt.

I looked at myself in the blackness of the dresser mirror and summoned the faces of those who had been there before me. But I saw only silence and darkness. I took a final shot of myself in the fly-specked mirror and lowered the camera.

Closure. Stupid word.

Halloumi Detox
by Christine Miscione

DO YOU WANT TO LOSE WEIGHT?
ARE YOU INTERESTED IN TRADITIONAL HEALTH?
HAVE YOU HAD ENOUGH OF YOUR HUMDRUM LIFE?

Do you want to cleanse yourself of every North American toxin that currently riddles your person? Do you want to lose that bulge of Christmas-excess, that perma-bloating, those unchristened lumps? Are you interested in health, wellness and amazing ancient customs?

If you answered yes to any of the above questions then HALLOUMI DETOX is for you!!

The Untold Greek Myth

Halloumi spilled from Aphrodite's crotch like sea foam as she waddled out of the Mediterranean and bathed on the shores of Cyprus. Nestled between her nourishing thighs, the Halloumi bathed there too, unripened and thick, developing its white sheen from the hot Grecian sun. As the Halloumi began to swell, Aphrodite took some to her beautiful lips and ate it. Liking the taste, she ate more and more until it burst from her mouth into the vague shape of man. Aphrodite ate that too and then, seeing a poor toothless peasant, Aphrodite scooped Halloumi from her loins and gave some to him as a generous gift. Soon the peasant's whole family ate of the sacred Halloumi, and they grew healthy and prosperous. From then on, Halloumi has been the secret panacea of the Mediterranean, a milky white elixir, Aphrodite's only kiss.

Great News!

We **HAVE** that Halloumi. We have attained the secret recipe from the descendent of the toothless peasant, a kind Mouflon farmer who lives along the crest of Mount Olympus. He has entrusted us with only the **purest** of Halloumis, and we would like to share this **ancient cure** with you.

Located in quaint Dundas, Ontario, one hour from the hustle and bustle of Toronto, our state-of-the-art **Alpha Mega Facility** is sure to meet your needs. Physicians, nurses, healers, and Grecian shamans are on staff. Seven- or fourteen-day detoxification programs available. Other programs available upon request.

Call us now! – 1-HALUM-YRSLF

Seven pounds is something nurses scream when hospital scales ladle newborns. Seven pounds of ground kidney for the meat pies, seven pounds of Christmas pudding made by Grandma Marg. Seven pounds was not the amount Dolores Nather hoped to gain over the yuletide season. Three days after champagne and New Year wishes, Dolores's bare feet un-stick sadly from the bathroom scale. The last few weeks rush back: seven pounds of innards dredged from the cavity of a Christmas turkey. Seven pounds of over-seasoned stuffing pushed back in. Seven pounds of shortbread cookies and mincemeat pie. Seven pounds of gingerbread decorated with seven pounds of snowflake confetti and snowmen jujubes. Seven pounds of festivities, of Christmas tinsel hanging precariously around her stomach, and not even the prunes of seven pounds of sugarplums can expunge what she's amassed.

Stanley Nather, Dolores's dear husband and recent survivor of male breast cancer, lost just over seven pounds during his mastectomy. For obvious reasons he had everything cut off such that now at least seven pounds of fluid sacs hang around his armpits and down to his hands like a flaccid hammock. Stanley has to take a Tamoxifen pill daily and he wears a specially designed nude-coloured compression sleeve on both arms so tight it pushes the fluid up against gravity and lets it drain into the ether. Dolores has accepted this fact of life: lose seven pounds during surgery, gain it all in bodily sewage. But when Dolores demands Stanley stand naked three separate times on the bathroom scale in order to confirm its competence, she nearly has a heart attack when it reads FOURTEEN POUNDS accrued in all the places of her dear husband's body, not just a mere seven.

"See, Dolor, working just fine."

"What do you mean it's working just fine? It says you've gained an extra seven pounds!"

Stanley, dear husband Stanley, frowns as he tries to make out the scale digits through his macular-degenerative eyes. Standing there, his naked body resembles a forgotten Santa sack filled with too many presents, lopsided and lumpy.

"Well, so it has, so it has."

"So it has? Is that all you have to say? We've both gained exactly seven pounds, that can't be right now can it? Something is off kilter, Stan, and I'm going to find out exactly what this nonsense is about!"

Unfortunately every one of the nine bathroom scales on which Dolores thereafter stands naked reads the same thing: SEVEN POUNDS of jolly jingle, SEVEN POUNDS of elf noses in a great big gut stocking. Seven pounds for her, seven pounds for Stanley, and between them fourteen pounds of collective yuletide blubber. But Dolores refuses to believe it. To her there are a plethora of plausible conspiracies. For instance, the nation-wide tampering of commercial scales such that the Canadian government can substantiate its claims of epidemic obesity. Or the conspiring of bathroom scale manufacturers to tamper with their own product in order to convince the public of epidemic obesity. Or the probable force-field surrounding the Nathers' residence acting as a kind of invisible tamperer, rearranging the circuitry of all bathroom scales for no particular reason other than the promotion of epidemic obesity.

It is during the application of one of Stanley's custom-made post-mastectomy compression sleeves that Dolores is struck with revelation. If you were a fly on the wall of the Nathers' master bedroom, you'd see a naked Stanley sitting with a green sleeve made of windbreaker material on one arm, a nude-coloured compression sleeve pulled snugly over top of it, and Dolores in her cotton teddy bear nightgown kneeling beside him yanking at a strap hanging from the green sleeve near his hands. You'd then see her pull harder and faster, hear the green apparatus whir, watch as it flies into the air like a kite, leaving behind only the compression sleeve strapped to Stanley's arms like an inverted spandex vacuum forcing juice up and out. Then you'd see her shoot up in the air unexpectedly, the green fabric still flying around behind her, you'd see her start stamping her foot maniacally, hear her yell "Phooey, phooey, *PHOOEY*!" over and over as she remembers again, for the last time, the double chocolate cinnamon snaps. The haystack frosties. The marzipan shaped as Christmas trees, and all that buttered squash! And buttered corn! And butter balls topped with red and white sprinkles! And the chocolate liqueurs every night after dinner, the wine and sedentariness, the lack of cheerful Christmas singing but instead listening to someone else sing carols as she stuffed her face with truffles and scotch. She and Stanley gained seven pounds of holiday lard. There is no conspiracy, no denying that fact.

By some mythical Grecian fate, the Halloumi Detox flyer, which arrived the day before, sits solitarily on the carpet of the Nathers' bedroom, adjacent to where Dolores is furiously stomping. Amid Stanley's attempts at calming Dolores and her repetitious PHOOEY, there is something of a wind that sends the flyer skyward, flittering in the air.

"Huh?" Dolores grabs at the aviator, wrestling it to the ground. "What the..." A few seconds pass, then "Stan, hunny, look here, look at this flyer. This might be just what we're looking for!"

ς

Two wheelchairs covered in images of Greek gods greet Dolores and Stanley at the entrance of the Alpha Mega Facility. Plucked mandolin music plays softly in the background as they're wheeled to the facility's clinic. An entire armamentarium there with a board-certified physician, Dr. Ned Hyundi, specialist in proctology, and a black cat sprawled across the treatment table. Greetings. Handshakes. Then tongue depressors checking for tonsillar calculi in the tonsil crypt. Sphygmomanometer's cuff around their arms, blood pressure normal. Needles produce little vials and blood results are adequate. Hearts checked. Stomachs measured. Weight recorded. Bodies lathered and showered in salt water. Feet sized and fitted into weightless white cotton slippers. Clothes removed and replaced with free-flowing white muumuus.

The Nathers have the full work-up. According to evaluative tests, everything about their constitutions is normal, and Dr. Ned Hyundi doesn't seem the least bit concerned about Stanley's fluid sacks, his need for compression sleeves or the Tamoxifen pill necessary for his survival. "Just small details," Dr. Ned Hyundi says, stroking the cat's head. "No contraindication between the detox program and wearing compression sleeves or that Tamoxifen pill. You might expel more of the drug than appropriate but it's my professional estimation that seven days without the full dose over the course of five years on the drug is nothing to worry about. The benefits of the program far outweigh the risks here."

After the medical assessment, the Nathers are led through a long corridor peppered with large doors and signs. Room 104: *FETA FALLOPIAN CLEANSE.* Room 105: *WHISPERING OLIVE MENTAL RECLAMATION.* Room 106's door is slightly open—*GYRO RECTAL SWEEP*—and inside, a large hunk of meat is outfitted with suction cups and wires. Every few seconds a ZAP and the meat jerks. Beside it, a massive gyrating pita roll propped vertically by metal prongs. The prongs stick into the pita's midsection and extend towards a rattling platform that looks like the body of a vegetable steamer.

"Stan hunny, look. They've got *jeye*rows in there," Dolores says, pointing.

"Well, isn't that something, Dolor."

Soon they reach Room 114: *HALLOUMI DETOX*, and a pretty Greek woman is there to greet them. "Hello Mr. and Mrs. Nather, I am Ms. Egli Hadjineophytou. I am the Halloumi Detox program director here at Alpha Mega. Come on in, have a seat."

Dolores and Stanley follow her into the room. Around them: myriad renderings of Aphrodite with creamed Halloumi thighs, white filing cabinets, a large white desk, white walls, white ceramic tiles of various sizes, and a glass door at the far end with a sign that reads *PURITY TESTING. AUTHORIZED PERSONNEL ONLY.* Dolores and Stanley sit down in two white wrought-iron chairs facing the desk.

"I meet all our newcomers when they arrive," Ms. Egli says. "I always like to inquire as to why they have come and what they hope to achieve during their Halloumi Detox. So…" She picks up a white clipboard and pen, writes something quickly. "So, why have you come to join us here at Alpha Mega?"

"Well, you see I've gained some seven pounds over the Christmas holidays," Dolores says, grabbing hold of her stomach for effect, yanking at it a bit too, "and my dear Stan here, he's gained the same amount."

"I see, so you'd like to lose weight. And how much do you hope to lose over the duration of the detox?"

"Well I'd like to go back to the size I was when I got married. Would you believe it, I was a size six on my wedding day. Size *six*!"

"Ok," Ms. Egli scribbles something. "And you, Mr. Nather? How much are you hoping to lose, ideally?"

"Oh, I don't know, I—"

"Well it would be nice if he lost all that holiday weight," Dolores interjects, "and even better if he could lose that excess fluid, right Stan?"

Stanley nods.

"Well you're in the right place. The Halloumi Detox program is renowned for its ability to systemically detoxify the body, cleansing all organs. That fluid you've accumulated, Mr. Nather, is to the best of my knowledge nothing more than the toxic by-products of your cancer treatment, in combination with the waste our bodies are forced to produce as a result of our North American lifestyles. Would you say you're a heavy eater, Mr. Nather?"

"Uh, yes he is."

Stanley nods.

"And how many times, on average, would you say you inhale in any given day?"

"Well you haven't thought of that before, have you Stan?"

Stanley shakes his head.

"None of us do, Mr. Nather, and that's the problem. It's very uncommon to consider inhalation quantity, but our research shows that with every inhalation, ninety-five percent of what we are taking into our bodies is highly toxic pollution. Thus as expected, inhalation quantity correlates with systemic pollutant quantity. It's a scientifically proven link. And to make matters worse, our data shows that we are actually inhaling at a greater rate than our ancestors. There simply isn't enough real oxygen in the air to sustain us."

"Well you know, Ms. Egli, my Stan *has* had some breathing problems over the last few years. He's been getting out of breath easier and starts to breathe very rapidly afterward, right Stan?"

Stanley nods.

"I see. Yes, even shallow inhalations can cause pollution to enter the bloodstream, just having that toxic air in our mouths is cause for worry. And Mr. Nather," Ms. Egli flips through a few pages on her clipboard. "Hmmm, yes, Mr. Nather, would you say the build-up of fluid in your upper body, is it hot or cold?"

"Cold. It's cold," Dolores responds.

Stanley nods.

"Cold. OK. Just one moment." Ms. Egli glides her finger down a page on her clipboard, eyes moving back and forth reading, "Cold, cold. Alright, uh-huh. Yes. I think for you, Mr. Nather, I would like to see you start on our Alpha Mega Halloumi Detox Supreme Program. This one is an intensified version of our standard program for newcomers who, like you, have fluid that is both visible and cold. This will consist of double-dosing your Halloumi intake."

Stanley nods.

"And for you, Mrs. Nather, I'd recommend only the standard Halloumi Detox Program. Your concerns of, if I heard correctly, *weight loss* will be easily met with the standard regimen."

"Are you sure I shouldn't go on that supreme one too? I mean, I'd like to lose a lot of weight here, *look* at this fat." Dolores grabs her stomach again and shakes it violently.

"No, I don't think your case warrants that, Mrs. Nather. We've successfully treated newcomers on the standard program who have had aspirations to lose more than you."

"Really?"

"All the time, Mrs. Nather. We average sixty people in and out of here each week and our success rate is close to one hundred percent."

"Well how exactly does the Halloumi Detox program work then?" Dolores inquires.

Ms. Egli puts her clipboard on her lap and folds her hands on top of it. "Did you read the ad, Mrs. Nather? All the pertinent information is in the ad."

"I did, but I would like to understand it at a deeper level."

"Well, Mrs. Nather, the Halloumi is an ancient cure of Cyprus. There is scientific evidence that shows it was literally born out of Aphrodite's loins. There have been fossils found that prove this fact and locals swear by it. They are very healthy people, the Cypriots, and much of their health can be attributed to Halloumi consumption. In fact, those Cypriots who have the misfortune of lactose intolerance and other milk allergies simply are not as healthy as the ones who can actively eat Halloumi. Does this make sense?"

"Yes, of course," Dolores says.

Stanley nods.

"Now, for your convenience, we offer a complimentary mouthguard to be worn every night of the program. This, we find, is essential to easing most of the clenching side effects of the detox. You'll be fitted for that after we're done here. And you're free to make use of the facility however you please. There are oxygen tents at your disposal. These are not mandatory, but are certainly useful in cleansing the air passages of any residual toxins. There is an extra fee for their use, but it is minimal in comparison to the benefits. Also, for a successful program, you're to stay within this section of the building at all times. It's been sealed off from most external toxins. Our meal times are on the regular schedule of breakfast, lunch, and dinner. We eat together, and meals consist only of quadruple-filtered water and of course Halloumi in various forms. Do you have any questions or concerns?"

Dolores shakes her head.

"Now Mr. and Mrs. Nather, there are some common and benign side effects to be aware of. In general the Halloumi Detox is very safe and we rarely have a problem. But you must realize that this program involves an entire colon cleansing, which means you can expect to be in the bathroom quite a bit. That's all part of the process, nothing to worry about at all. Keep hydrated and you won't experience any of the headaches or fainting spells some of our newcomers have experienced in the past. There is purified water flowing at all times from our replica Spili fountains located at the back of the building. You can also go to the dining room whenever you please and access the same water there. Does this sound good?"

"Yes."

"And hearing the rules and the common side effects, knowing in full what you might expect during the program, do you both wish to proceed?"

"Yes we do."

Stanley nods.

"Excellent." Ms. Egli hands Dolores the clipboard. "I'll get you to please sign here, here and here. After that's complete, I'll show you to your room."

ς

Day one at the Alpha Mega facility: creamed Halloumi porridge. Fried Halloumi cakes. Halloumi smoothie. Halloumi cookies. Popped Halloumi during the nighttime Cypriot sing-along. Dolores is on the toilet for two hours in the early evening. Stanley is handling his double-dose just fine.

ς

Day two. Oxygen tents. Twenty-five cents for five minutes. Slip the coins in the machine like a dryer at the laundromat. Lie down inside. Rest your head on the pillow and simply breathe. *Breathe.* Inhale that pure air. Feel that clean oxygen hit your throat and lungs, filling every cell of your body with nourishment. Imagine sunsets over the Mediterranean. Wild Grecian air. Imagine bathing your internal organs with ancient nutrition, enrobing every molecule of your being with the decadence of Cypriot purity.

After oxygen tents there are Halloumi popsicles for an afternoon snack. Dinner: scalloped Halloumi with grated Halloumi sprinkled on pan-seared Halloumi steak. Warm Halloumi pie for dessert. Stanley feels slightly queasy and notices his mouth clenching, decides to wear his mouthguard during the evening sing-along. When asked how she feels, Dolores responds with "Spunky." She only spent one hour on the toilet today.

ς

Day three begins with Halloumi Benedict for breakfast. Dolores tells Stanley not to worry about wearing the compression sleeves for the rest of the week. According to her, Halloumi Supreme is doing wonders for the sacking of his fluid. "Fluid dissolution!" she cries. "Toxic junk evaporation!"

After the evening Cypriot sing-along—in between hours of white liquid outpourings in the bathroom—Dolores and Stanley are both feeling frisky, re-ignite fires on the white sheets of their Halloumi-shaped bed. Dolores feels thinner too. She hasn't weighed herself yet; the mid-program weigh-in comes tomorrow. But she swears her stomach is shrinking, and she sprawls across the bed buck-naked, purring at Stanley as he undresses.

"Oh Stan hunny, I just love you. I just love you so much," Dolores says, kissing his thighs. "Oh, Stan dear."

ς

Day four, the weigh-in. Dolores and Stanley swept away on wheelchairs to the clinic at 6am. They strip down. Bare feet press scale platforms and Dolores comes in at ten pounds lost, Stanley is down seventeen.

"My lord, Stan, do you see that? I *told* you your fluid was disappearing! Didn't I tell you that?"

"Well gosh! You were right, Dolor, you were exactly right."

Dolores gives Stanley a wink, then turns to the attendant. "I think you'd better get us smaller muumuu robes. Look at those numbers! We're smaller than when we arrived."

"I am happy for your loss, Mrs. Nather. But so sorry, our robes only come in one-size-fits-all."

After being swept back to their bedroom on the same wheelchairs, the Nathers get it on in the shower. Ten seconds post-climax, Dolores runs to the toilet and spends the next hour there, nearly misses breakfast. After all that sewage loss, feeling even thinner than before, she sashays into the dining hall, her muumuu robe safety-pinned tightly at the back and hugging her rediscovered hourglass curve. "Stan hunny, thank you for waiting for me before eating. You're a doll, a real sweetheart. What do you think of my dress?"

Soon both are filled with inglorious amounts of Halloumi homefries, sunnyside up Halloumis, Halloumi waffles and spreads, Halloumi muffins. Stanley forces down four glasses of Halloumi-shake, feels his mouth clench, bones lock, all the muscles of his face tightening. After breakfast, he and Dolores ask Ms. Egli about it.

"Oh, only a bruxist side effect. Nothing to worry about, Mr. Nather. Very common for a man your age, especially on the Halloumi Detox Supreme Program and in combination with your Tamoxicyclops pills." Ms. Egli puts her hand on his shoulder for reassurance. "Really, there's no need to worry. Our data shows that as Halloumi is consumed, new flora is introduced to the gut and during this process of transition the body might become tense, causing bruxism. You could wear your mouthguard throughout the day if you'd like?"

"He'll do just that, won't you Stan dear?"

Stanley nods.

Then it's Stanley's turn in the bathroom. An afternoon staring at the Adonis statue on a pedestal by the sink. Three toilet paper rolls later, and Dolores and Stanley are back at it on their Halloumi bed, rolling around like it's their honeymoon.

"Stan hunny, I feel like we're nineteen again. Like those nights in the Bahamas, do you remember? That cement shack where they kept the pesticides, sneaking in there and making love without anyone noticing?" Dolores traces Stanley's mastectomy scar with her ring finger. "And that club-footed room attendant! He was a hoot, wasn't he? Kept bringing us Bloody Marys whenever we got too loud!"

"Of course I remember, Dolor. It feels just like yesterday."

"Oh, Stan."

ς

Day five and Stanley continually readjusts his jaw. He's making out with Dolores before breakfast, uses both hands to realign his upper and lower mouth. While brushing his teeth, he knocks his joints back into place, every time a hideous cluck and bones grind.

"Don't worry about that, Stan. Like Ms. Egli said, it's a common bruxer side effect. It will go away after the transition is complete. Here, take your Tamoxifen and don't worry another second!"

Lunch rolls around, and Dolores's muumuu, still pinned, is now cut down the front, a large V with its point smack-dab between her two breasts. She leans over her platter of mini-Halloumi sandwiches and gives Stanley a wink. "All this is yours later tonight."

There were hours spent relaxing in the oxygen tents. An afternoon snack of corned Halloumi chunks. Dolores explodes in the bathroom afterward while Stanley inquires about an island of tiny chancre sores found underneath his tongue. By dinnertime both are energized; Dolores swaggering into the dining hall with the bottom hem of her muumuu cut away in a zigzag pattern, Stanley tagging along behind.

A dinner of battered Halloumi soup, blanched Halloumi with a side of mashed Halloumi. For dessert: deep-fried Halloumi cupcakes. Dolores and Stanley, filled to the gills, retreat to their bedroom for involuntary colonic irrigations in the toilet bowl followed by a romp under the bed sheets.

ҫ

Day six, Stanley's jaw won't open.

"Don't worry Stan hunny. It'll unclench in a few minutes. I promise. Should I wait for you before going for breakfast?"

Stanley scribbles his response on Alpha Mega stationery: *No, no, go for breakfast, Dolor. No use in us both being late.*

It doesn't take much to convince Dolores to eat. And with that, she leaves for the dining hall without her husband. A decision she will regret every day for the rest of her life.

"Good morning, Ms. Egli!" Dolores calls across the dining hall. "Oh, we're feeling wonderful. We are very energized, and look how skinny I'm getting!" Dolores tries yanking at her stomach. "It's just incredible! Barely anything there! Me and Stan just cannot *believe* tomorrow is our last day—it's snuck right up on us. We're thinking of signing on for another week!"

After breakfast, Dolores putters around, waiting for Stanley. Where is he? She checks the clock: thirty minutes since breakfast ended. Where is he? She decides to bring his food up to him.

To her room she prances, hips a-swaying, muumuu recalibrated sexily, platter in arms, Halloumi Jell-O with a big bowl of shredded Halloumi flakes and Halloumi smoothie. She knocks on the door with her foot. No answer. He's probably in the bathroom. Knocks one more time. Still nothing. She balances the platter on her hips, turns the doorknob then struts in.

"*Staaaanleeeeey?*"

The bathroom light is on, door closed, and a smell of antiquated cheese, weeping cheese, cheese torpedoing through idiopathic hospital sludge, cheese cobbled with the remnants of a bowel curetting. A smell so closely akin to what rots under a baboon's inflamed ass that Dolores is nearly knocked over, Halloumi Jell-O tub smashing on the ceramic tiles.

"Stan?" Her voice is quieter now. Apprehensive. A timid breath in, "Stan? ...*honey*?"

Dolores places the platter carefully on the bed. She sees Stanley's muumuu tangled among the bed sheets, his slippers placed neatly on his pillow. "Stan?" Then, in the corner of her eye, Dolores spots the tip of his foot poking out from the closet. Big toe. Baby toe. Poking. "STAN?" She rushes over, sees his body supine, fiercely stiff, arms pressed against his sides, legs perfectly straight. Notices his eyes open, both eyes staring in opposite directions, two repelled magnets.

"Oh my Lord! Stan, hunny... Stan, can you hear me?"

But something strange in the muzzle of Stanley's face. Something of a bone hinge forced too strongly upward, misaligning skull structure, making hard bulges around temples, knobs of bone where earlier there were none.

"Oh my…"

Stanley's jaw clenched tightly, clenched transgression, teeth going up and down into gum tissues, joints pushed out of cavities, eyes seemingly lower than usual. And a soft white powder.

"Oh my—Stan? *Hunny*? Can you hear me?"

Dolores rushes to the hallway. From her Halloumi-filled gut, loud unadulterated wails so shrill ceramic tiles crack. From her loins—that tender place never spilling of velvety Halloumi but always loving a man like the great Aphrodite loved the sea, the island, the unripened brine of cream: "*STANLEEEEEEEYYYY!*"

ς

Day seven. The final day. Dolores with a massive Ziploc freezer bag full of Stanley's shit. The smell of abused ballet shoes smeared in two-hundred-year-old Halloumi. The smell of defogging a pile of xenophobic hork as Dolores clasps the bag at the top like she just won a goldfish at a carnival. She won't let anyone come near it.

Meanwhile Stanley is in the morgue, carted there after he clenched to the point of jawbones perforating brain lobes. Bone powder like cocaine embroidering his tongue. Bottom teeth straight through upper gums. Stanley is in the morgue completely gutted of liquids and food. There's nothing left for his innards to organize if they could, all switches turned off, empty stomach, desiccated kidneys, liver parched. Everything flew the coop, an unstoppable gush twenty minutes prior to death according to forensics, the toilet brimming. And Dolores, so desperate, used a complimentary coffee mug to scoop and scoop. The last living remnants of her dear husband Stanley.

ς

One week later, Dolores's credit card bill pays out two-thousand-and-seventy dollars to Alpha Mega, an extra fee added for not returning her white muumuu the same way she got it. Ms. Egli, sympathetic hostess, agrees not to charge Dolores for Stanley's shit-stained muumuu, the one he died in. She also doesn't charge Dolores for the impenetrable plastic bag to carry Stanley's last vestiges or the ruined coffee mug or the Adonis statue Dolores smashed on Dr. Ned Hyundi's desk.

"Shame on you, Dr. Ned Hyundi! You and your stupid coterie of Greek lords!"

Dr. Ned Hyundi feels no remorse. He strokes his cat trying to hold back a grin. What could he have possibly done wrong? He gave the Nathers the full medical work-up—everything was copasetic. So what that Mr. Nather recently had a mastectomy or took Tamoxifen daily? So what that Mr. Nather was full

of fluids because his lymph nodes failed at waste management? He, Dr. Ned Hyundi, did his job. He followed all mandates. He did exactly as he was told. But sympathy? Sympathy for a couple who would willingly pay exorbitant fees for needless luxury? A greedy sucker is born every day, and no, Dr. Ned Hyundi will not feel sorry for the Nathers.

Dolores has no grounds to sue Alpha Mega (she signed the waiver, she gave her consent); she can do nothing but pay the fee for the program and bury dear Stanley as per his legal wishes. But she still has Stanley in the plastic bag. Excrement, and she brings it everywhere. The bath. The kitchen. The grocery store. At night, Stanley sleeps on the pillow beside hers. In the morning, scones and clotted cream with dear Stanley. Dolores wants Stanley with her at every second of the day and would've continued that way, carrying him around, if it wasn't for the smell—that malodorous eggnog, that waft of belligerent sputum.

So, naturally Dolores takes to reason. All Stanley ate for the last week of his life was Halloumi. Every meal Halloumi. Every snack Halloumi. All he drank was water. He did take a Tamoxifen pill daily, but that's negligible like the water. Here are Stanley's remains. Here is Stanley in a bag mixed with watery Halloumi.

And suddenly, out of the Grecian ruins of her innocent weight-loss dream, an equation emerges, a formula so obvious she wonders why she never thought of it before: *Shit = Stanley + Halloumi + (Tamoxifen pill + water x 0).* And if *Shit = Stanley + Halloumi + (Tamoxifen pill + water x 0),* then *Shit - Halloumi - (Tamoxifen pill + water x 0)= Stanley.*

The difference can only be Stanley.

Swift as Halloumi through the digestive track, she enlists the help of a vacuum specialist. She plops Stanley down on an operating table, plastic tubes and mechanical gadgets surrounding him. Then Halloumi is sucked like liposuction from Stanley's shit, white-yellowy emancipation. And then seven pounds. Seven pounds of Stanley left over after the extraction. Seven pounds of Stanley preserved with formaldehyde globs in a miniature Grecian-inspired totem pole sitting on her mantle, his two nude-coloured compression sleeves dangling beside. Then one day Dolores wants more, needs to invigorate her Stanley with greater movement and life. So she dresses Stanley, who by this time has shrunk from seven to six pounds, in a designer scuba-suit made only of his compression sleeves and impenetrable rubber, and keeps him—for the rest of his life—as an aquatic Halloumi-shaped glob, floating in an aquarium beside her bed.

Roasted with White Truffle
by Arley Sorg

Alicia Martinson marvelled at Jessie's ability to scream without knowing he was screaming. Or at least to deny that the screaming had happened. He likened himself to other Michelin chefs with abrupt tempers. After testing it through several television interviews, he officially coined his own phrase: "Just the right amount of salt in the wound! Just what's warranted!"

Jessie Strand chased another would-be hero off the Infamy loading dock. "You stink like goat's piss!" he yelled, then scowled at the bloody footprints tracked through the restaurant's back lot. He turned to Alicia. His faded, choppy mohawk bristled, and she knew what was next. She raced down the hall to the mop closet and grabbed a mop and a bucket of soapy water. By the time she returned, she could tell his anger had been sated with her response.

He liked one thing more than yelling. He liked seeing people jump, already knowing what was expected of them.

"I know that look." Jessie pretended to be hurt. His eyes wanted to do the hurting. "I'm not as bad as a certain Scottish chef we know. Nor as picky as a certain Frenchman I could name."

Alicia knew this trap. Jessie had many traps. Navigating the mine-laden seas of his moods was one of several requirements in the long path to sous-chefdom. Along with cleaning drains, mopping, and anything else that needed doing. Since she'd been promoted only two months prior, she kept her lips shut and worked up a quick sweat. Her jaw flexed harder than a heel of stale bread.

The dejected hero Araweden cast baleful glances back. As if he might pry open the doors to Infamy once again. He tossed the black sack of meat into the back of his rust-speckled VW and sped off. Bright red drips flecked the road behind him, slipping biohazardously from the seam of his trunk.

No morning was complete without at least one hopeful cook sprinting out of the kitchen, smothering their face in the crook of their arm.

"Are you paying attention, Alice?" Jessie made a game of not quite using a person's actual name.

"Yes, Chef!" But she wasn't paying attention. She stared at the sauté pan, in all its crackling fury, her ears focused past the produce sink and stretched after Cora's sobbing. Alicia's heart contracted in time to Cora's sorrow.

"Good. Meat, in. Quickly! Oil is smoking!" Jessie also adopted a strange European affect, with a sprinkle of effeminate gesticulation, despite the fact that he was born in Denver and was religiously heterosexual.

Alicia laid the filet in the pan. Pops of oil stung her knuckles.

"What," he put his fists on his hips and reared up. Chest puffed out, he was nearly her height. "Is the secret to drake?"

Her mind roiled. She was still thinking about Cora. This was her fault. She'd helped Cora get hired. Like a fool, the girl had been grateful. Cora showed her gratitude with a dinner, a bottle of good wine, and a romp that lasted the better part of the evening. Naturally, they pretended to be professional at work. "Ummm."

"C'mon, Alice. I don't have all day." Jessie slammed his palms against the metal counter. "What is the secret to cooking drake!"

"Hot pan, baste, and—"

"Gods, you're going to *kill* someone! Poison from the female's fangs!"

"Ah!"

"Poison relaxes the muscles, and the flame remnants will leach out into the sauce, becoming inert! Alice, pay attention! The customer's mouth will *scorch* if you don't use the poison!"

"Won't the poison—"

"Argh! Get out! I can't deal with you right now!" He gave her a little shove—hard enough to humiliate, not hard enough for a lawsuit. "Alice!" he called, stopping her at the doorway. Her feet were already eager to chase after Cora. "Olive oil, Alice! It counteracts drake poison! Gods. Go home. Get out."

She found Cora crying on the front steps. Alicia knew that *get out* translated to *come crawling back in a few minutes*. She wasn't sure that Cora knew this, and if Cora actually left she wouldn't have a job tomorrow.

Behind them two boys in black vests and black pants put all they had into cleaning glass doors. Both were pimply enough to be below the legal age to work.

"You have to go back," Alicia told Cora, waving at the smoke from her cigarette. "You have to apologize."

"Wait," Cora pouted. For a heartbeat, she pricked some strange lust in Alicia. Something about her puffy red eyes and those glistening tears. Alicia usually went for strong women and weak men, and she didn't have time for commitment. But she eyed Cora's trembling lower lip and wondered how much time she could get away with, before Jessie would send someone after her.

"I have to apologize to *him*?"

"Yeah. Of course. Ostensibly for being stupid. And use those words. Minus the *ostensibly*."

"That's fu— "

"Yeah, I know. But this place is going to be packed tonight. Packed on a Tuesday, Cora. He's a jerk but he's one of the best."

A hero struggled towards them, strained to tow a massive black sack. "Not *one of*." He flashed a typically charming grin. Most heroes had that charisma. Alicia supposed it was why she preferred *weak* men. Heroes were annoying. "He *is* the best."

"Gods." Alicia stood and brushed her hands on her apron. "I know you aren't bringing some carcass through the front. And I know you aren't fouling my parking lot with that trail of blood!"

He jerked his head to flick his long black hair from his face, then leaned in conspiratorially. Muck smeared his boots, and his sword scabbard was soaked with—probably—guts. "White behemoth!"

Cora shot up. "Gods!"

Alicia felt her skin turn clammy. "That's highly illegal."

"And *dangerous*," the hero straightened, drenched in practiced smug.

"Does—" Alicia paused, wondered if she really wanted to know. "Does Jessie know?"

"Strand's the one requested it!" The hero pulled the sack open just enough for Alicia to peer in. The behemoth's three elegant white horns were stained red.

"It's a *female*!" Alicia's heart was a firemoth in her chest. "Gods, that's—"

"Special guests, Strand said. So you letting me in?"

"No! Yes, I mean. Around the back. Are you daft?" An army of options marched through Alicia's skull. Led by a standard bearer that flapped *run*. Platoons in gleaming mail stomped various legal risks as well as the various possible ways to turn Jessie in. General Ethics shouted into her brain: white behemoths were endangered, killing a female was especially grave. Despite the fanfare, when her mind quieted, she remembered her years of culinary school, the two clumsy and emotionally dreadful trysts she'd let herself fall into primarily to make connections, and her year of scrubbing pots. Followed by her year of being a prep cook.

All to rise to *this* position.

She had really worked so hard! A 50-hour week was a slow week. And she had learned more about food after becoming sous-chef than she had learned in all the other years combined. Besides, she reasoned, she'd seen Jessie break the law before—seen him squeeze lemon juice into the eyes of the rules. A couple more years and she would be able to open her own place. It would be an automatic success. She just needed patience.

By the time her thinking was done, Alicia was alone on the stoop. Cora had returned to the kitchen and the sky had darkened. Faces poached red with sweat and work, the boys dragged mop buckets from the parking lot. The behemoth's blood had been wiped clean.

ς

"Cora!" Jessie shouted through a slimy grin, somewhere between disdain and lust. "Cora, move your ass! Sides for two boar."

"Yes, Chef!"

"Alice! Quick! To the pass, please."

Friday night had come. Jessie had a very special menu planned for a charity event. Few restaurants in the world could serve the sort of fare on offer at Infamy. Heroes were as dwindling a species as their quarry. But Jessie had a knack for contracting the best heroes, and the best heroes had a knack for finding the rarest sorts of proteins.

Unfortunately, Jessie loved to push his protégés. An individual would either soar and prove what a great mentor Jessie was, or they would crash and he would relish the wounding. Not to mention salting of said wounds. He liked to throw them into the deep end and wait for them to drown.

Three chefs in the world, no more, were said to be able to prepare basilisk without mortal repercussions to themselves, their co-workers or, if the dish made it so far, to the customer. Yet Jessie had somehow acquired the dangerous meat and had stepped off the line to expedite, leaving Alicia alone at the stove, basilisk brain broiling in a pan, three basilisk tails in the salamander, and two loins seared on one side in cast-iron skillets. He left one of the skull caps, glassy eyes staring at the tiled wall, sitting in a sheet pan on the counter, with little instruction as to what he intended for it.

"Alice! To the pass!" Jessie repeated. His arms were crossed. Everyone knew that was the dampness of air before a very violent squall.

Recipes and rules collided with hot dangers. Even touching the skull could turn her to stone. Any piece of meat was so poisonous, if not handled *precisely*, the venom would corrupt the very metal of a utensil, creep into the body and…

Damn that's it! Alicia felt a sliver of the hero's smug and plucked wooden tongs from the wall. "Two minutes, Chef!" she called, making sure everyone heard the capital C in the tone of her voice.

When dinner service concluded, Jessie glowered and watched his brigade clear down. "Not a speck, not a spot!" he called out. He rose periodically, inspected, pointed at short-comings, and returned to his seat.

For Alicia, the routine was a bitter meal. At the same time, he was *right*. His palate was extraordinary, his eye for detail was meticulous. His plates dazzled, and his kitchen stayed *spotless*.

The clearing-down done, he gave each employee in turn their permission to leave. All except for Alicia.

She watched Cora linger in the doorway, a mischievous look perked on her lips. At the start of their shift, Cora had thanked her for coming to get her. "I might have left," she said, then whispered into Alicia's ears—right there next to a prep cook deboning wyvern wings—"Come by later, I should thank you properly."

At the time, Alicia had no intention of a late-night foray. But seeing the heated twinkle of Cora's eye, her confident flirtation, her half-smile and cocky tilt of head…well. It had been a good day so far, no reason not to make it a good night.

"Well done today, Alice." Jessie crossed his arms and smiled, snatching Alicia's attention. She heard the exit doors open, hesitate. Then close after a long moment. "Are you listening?"

He'd said something and she'd missed it. Cursing herself, she stared at the tiles.

"I said, I thought you'd die! Aren't you shocked?"

He thought I'd die? Was he trying to kill me? "Umm."

"I'm pleasantly surprised. You are, without a doubt, the best sous-chef I've had in years. And that's saying something."

"Umm. Thanks." Pride and pleasure mixed with distaste and fear. It was an off-putting cocktail that set her body on edge.

"Tomorrow night there's a party. Very exclusive, very secret. Luminaries, all. I won't give names, but let's just say three movie stars, two musicians, and a minor god."

"Wait. A god? I thought—"

"They keep it discreet, but they're out there. Interested? Or shall I ask someone else to help me?"

"No. Yes. Hells yes!" Alicia made herself grin. Her cheeks were instantly sore.

"Good. It's a secret. No one will know. In a week or two, naturally the dinner will be leaked to the press, but not the details. Tell. No. One." He took the liberty of placing his index finger over her lips in a *shush* gesture. His hand smelled of sweat, curry and sex. Alicia wanted to retch. For the sake of her career, she nodded and smiled. She channelled what she could remember of being wide-eyed with wonder.

ҁ

"To monsters!" Jessie toasted the room.

Alicia had only heard of suites like this one. Near the top floor of the most exclusive downtown hotel. Sauna in the middle of the living room, television nearly as long as her compact car, a patio big enough to house a family. It made her dizzy and eager.

When she'd first entered, she stared stupidly at the guests, until Jessie pinched her arm.

Jessie's one true rival, Andre Rathdowne, had already arrived. He also had three carts of ingredients, not to mention an assistant.

What Alicia hadn't expected was that Jessie and Andre were there as competitors. The various stars were judges. The last time they had competed, the judges were split like a bad sauce, and a brawl ensued. Two judges were hospitalized and Jessie had a broken nose. Since then, Jessie had publicly declared he would no longer compete.

The suite had two closed-off separate kitchens. Before starting prep, the chefs posed in front of the stars to make a toast. After Jessie's brief words, Andre gave a long speech about the metaphor of cookery as the cycles of life. At first, several onlookers nodded, smiled, even laughed. Soon eyes were glazed and smiles were stiff.

"Which one is the god?" Alicia whispered, analyzing every feature of their guests.

"You are really hopeless," Jessie said through his teeth. "Twelve guests. Eliminate the ones you know. And the one that's left is?"

"The god," Alicia said, stung. *Should be used to it by now.*

After toasts they sped to their kitchens. Jessie unveiled small sacks of exquisite, exotic proteins, and even a few monstrous plants that were extremely dangerous and hard to find. Her stomach turned when he opened the last small sack: a clutch of warrenbirds, ducklings at that.

"But they..."

Jessie frowned. She felt as if the temperature dropped ten degrees. Satisfied that he'd frowned her into submission, he started unloading onto counters. Alicia crossed her arms. She couldn't stop her head shaking *no.* It took several moments for Jessie to notice.

His face reddened and his mohawk shivered. "Am I cooking on my own tonight?"

"I can't! They're *sentient*!"

He sucked air and gripped the side of a cart. "*All* these monsters are sentient! Do you think you're respecting the ingredient by whining?"

"No." She tried to be strong, to emulate her first real lover, Amanda. The way Amanda would stick out her jaw, the way she'd make fists and glare, as if to say *I can hit just as hard as you can.* Alicia's voice broke. "They are *really* sentient! They have language, they have culture!"

"They're *monsters*! Gods, Alice. Look at them! Birds with human faces? I mean, have you *tasted* them? So delicate..."

Alicia gripped her belly, shuffled to a shiny sink, and proceeded to make a big, splashing mess.

"Unbelievable." Jessie sounded more dumbfounded than angry. "You're just an amateur!"

She wiped her mouth with a paper towel and stretched her back, reforming the image of Amanda in her mind. "It's not right! They're endangered. And they *speak* for gods' sake!"

"Yes, yes. It's illegal and blah blah blah. Do you think a god would eat it if it's wrong?" Jessie pointed at the door, as if any moment a god would shimmer into being and grant a host of wishes.

"They're *children*!"

"The proper term is *ducklings*. And I assure you, I had the hero kill the entire family. Just so no one would miss them. It was the humane thing to do."

Heat steamed through Alicia's limbs. Hate coated her tongue along with the bile. Gripping her elbows, she stared at her knives, snug in their black cloth case. Each one just so sharp, each one just so capable of ending this madness.

"Alicia," Jessie grunted. She startled out of her rage at the sound of her actual name. "You're almost there, little girl. You have the same dream we all have. I had it, and I will never speak of the horrors I endured to get here. Cling to your dreams, little girl. Don't throw your life away."

Shadows made his eyes seem hollow. The *little girl* bit was a knife on glass, and it took all she had to keep from cringing. Still. She breathed and let his words soak in. Not to mention the fact that he'd used her *actual name.*

And like so many times, as much as he was a hateful bastard, she decided he was right. She nodded her assent. She also decided he wouldn't get the satisfaction of verbal agreement. "But I'm not touching those things. Not in any way."

"Gods! Alright," he smirked. And they set about cooking to the very reaches of their abilities.

ς

They were to take turns, Jessie and Andre, to present complete meals. The first set of three courses was Jessie's. Dish after dish, Alicia cooked, garnished and helped carry foods the likes of which even she had never seen. She was astonished by Jessie's unbridled speed and skill. It was as if the restaurant were a hobby. His true culinary powers were secrets he had never revealed. Until this very night.

Although the foamy loathing in her was somewhat washed away by his skill, not to mention the rigour of the work, it was renewed when the warrenbirds were presented. She hung back by the door, sneering as Jessie served the guests himself. When all was done, he snapped a command for Alicia to go clear everything down. "It's the least you can do, for your sour attitude," he murmured, just out of earshot of who Alicia thought might be the god.

Jessie mingled with guests, laughed, gorged on praise, clapped shoulders and sipped champagne. Alicia slipped into the kitchen, rolled up her sleeves, and eyed her knives, wondering if she'd missed the best opportunity to rid the world of the cancer known as Jessie Strand. *Crime of passion*, she would argue to the courts. *Ask any of them! Ask the god! Jessie deserved it!*

Jessie had freely made a mess. It was unusual of him, and Alicia reckoned he'd probably planned to make her life miserable all along. She scrubbed for over two hours. Her fingertips wrinkled while the sound of revellers rose and fell. Jessie's coarse laughter cut through it all.

When everything was rendered spotless enough to pass inspection, she washed her hands and her face, steeled her heart and strode back to the living room.

Possibly from the consumption of excess alcohol, the god's skin gave a faint red glow, and several notables were in casual embraces on couches and loveseats and tables with several other notables. *Like a bunch of college kids*, Alicia thought, lips pressed together. Clothes hadn't come off yet. The scents of Andre's round filled the room with rich smells.

"Do you enjoy monster?" a man said, strolling up to her. He had a weak chin and listless eyes, a bony slip of body revealed by the silk shirt unbuttoned to his navel. Hair seemed undecided on his chin. By the time he'd put the sparkling glass in her hand, she had already thought up several ways to both hurt him and make him pass out grinning.

"Depends. Sometimes. I like sea serpent. But you know, it's nearly impossible to get."

"So eating monster doesn't shock you? The liberals are calling for—"

Alicia blurred out his words. She would rather sip and dream than let him ruin her arousal. He laughed at something and she blinked back at him. Her eyes tickled along the open pathway of his shirt then lingered at his belt. She hoped he would get the message.

"This is the first Monster Meat party I've been to," he smiled like an alligator.

It was *all monster*, she realized, the champagne settling its slow effect into her skull. *Expensive.* She floundered between seizing the guy—whom she decided was a big movie star, far bigger than he probably was—and dragging him into the kitchen for a very rough quickie that would hopefully result in his being bruised and probably unconscious, and searching out her mentor and getting the hell out of there. There was an inspection to be had, and best get it over with.

The room had become smoky, low-lit. Her eyes strained through darkness, snagged on faces—and yes, here it goes, a few shirts had come off—but she couldn't find that irritating mohawk. Empty plates were scattered on the floor. Not the plates Jessie had brought. She guessed Andre's appetizers were already done.

"You know, I've been called a monster in the bedroom!" the not-so-bright star smiled.

Alicia rolled her eyes. She sucked the last of her champagne and left him holding the empty glass. It was definitely inspection time. Where was that ass?

"For my main," Andre chirped, sweeping through the kitchen door, "loin with champagne and chestnut gravy, roasted and served with white truffle, in its skull!"

His assistant lifted the cloche. Steam billowed into already dense air. A beautifully rich sauce teased at Alicia's nose. Pieces of meat were delicately layered in architecturally divine symmetry. All set in a skull whose faded but colourful mohawk shivered along the back of the dish.

Alicia's gut collapsed. Nausea clung to her throat. Most surprisingly, wetness itched her eyes and blurred the smoke-clotted room.

Luminaries stood and clapped. Smiles perked and sweaty bodies pried away from each other. Untangled kisses changed to laughter and cheers.

Alicia fell back against a wall. Numbness spread through her fingers. She brushed off a tear that had the nerve to crawl down her cheek.

"Ah! Delectable." The guy from earlier had found his way back to her side. She pushed off the wall and composed herself, unwilling to let skinny boy be the steady one. "You are the heir to the throne. Does this mean you have a new restaurant?" He set a refilled glass in her hand.

She tensed, sniffed back tears. She *was* the highest up, the sole heir to Jessie's gastronomic expertise. It would be days or weeks before anyone knew he was gone. He'd left the restaurant a few times before, inexplicably, only to return blustering and posturing as if nothing had happened.

If all went well…

"One of the greatest monsters of our time!" Andre bellowed. Lined up for his portion, a rock star pumped his fist in agreement.

Her belly mostly settled, she raised her glass in a half-hearted toast. Despite the crush in her chest, she couldn't help but smirk. "You know, you just might be right," she said, already rearranging the menu and thinking on which heroes she really didn't like. Oh yes, of course, let's promote Cora. If she can handle the heat.

Alicia pushed her shoulders back and arched up on her toes. It put her a good inch taller than skinny boy. She stared coolness at him, more satisfied to be wanted than to have. "I do think Infamy will be mine!"

The Feast of Father Gorger
by Samuel Marzioli

"Meal time—"

"Will commence—"

"Immediately," we said.

For fifty years we bided our time in the darkness of the vault of the earth, waiting for the culmination of our hunger. We had almost given in a decade ago, but we sated ourself with memories. Recollections of those cities we felled, glutted with a ripe human harvest, and the succulence of fear-seasoned meat. Now, the yearning burned within our shared stomach and we could restrain ourself no longer.

As we tore through the ground above us—ancient rock crumbling to dust from the force of each upward thrust—we argued over our initial destination.

"London and its tea-soaked citizens. The gristle made from proper English living."

"No! Tokyo and its rice-fed inhabitants. Wrapped in silk kimonos and suits, like human sushi."

"Mississippi and their pan-fried filth. Their ample, soft exteriors and their hard, crunchy centres."

And then we realized.

"We could—"

"Always try—"

"Them all!"

We punched a mile-wide hole through the earth's crust, just north of the English Channel, and slithered out under the harsh and sweltering sun. Though we were born a child of the dark, and it was blinding to our many eyes, it nourished life and afforded us our enduring pleasures. And so, our body rippled under its brilliant light in gratefulness.

We headed straight for London, anxious to cut a swath through the appetizer-counties that surrounded it. We released a gluttonous moan, the same kind that had on countless occasions filled entire armies with dread and driven weaker minds to insanity. In response, we expected to hear the wails of those acknowledging their coming torment, their inevitable deaths. But there was nothing, save the hum of the planet's vibrations and the soft caress of wind.

Along the way, we saw the devastation of the region. Buildings and habitations of all sorts levelled. Farmlands, forests and meadows pressed flat, imprinted with the remains of dead and dry vegetation. And when we came at last upon London itself, it was as if the entire city had been scooped out, leaving only a sopping crater.

"What—"

"Does this—"

"Mean?" we said.

As if in answer, a blaze erupted in the centre of the absent city, expanding into the vastness of a mountain. Towers of steam lifted and merged with the sporadic cloud cover above. And with each lurching step it made in our direction, the air quivered from its approach.

"Greetings, Father Gorger," he said, simmering low to the ground in supplication. "Is the Feasting upon us?"

"Conflagration, our fourth born."

"Who did this—"

"To our meal?"

As he considered our words, his plasma core shifted colours from red to blue to yellow. "It was Gormandizer. After he passed through this region, it never recovered."

Upon hearing the news, we grumbled inside, but held back our wrath. After all, a birthling was allowed to make a mistake now and again. When we first coalesced in the bowels of the earth, and rose to greet the dawn of the Triassic, we too withheld little during our first feasting. Munching every pelycosaur, archosaur, and therapsid we found.

"Our first-born—"

"Is one after—"

"Our own hearts!"

"More than you might think, Father," Conflagration said and vanished, leaving behind smoldering miles of red-hot silica.

We burrowed back into the ground. Using the ancient tunnel systems we'd carved eons before, we made our way east. The hunger increased within us and the ache transformed into pain that suffused our entire being. The moans we uttered then came from the suffering of want, not the pleasure of anticipation. One thing we knew for sure, there would be no toying with our meal upon our arrival. Only unmitigated consumption.

We lifted out of the Sea of Japan, groaning with the delight of our arrival. But even from the waters, our many eyes could see we'd come too late. The cities upon that shore had been snuffed into oblivion, and coursing farther inland showed us only much of the same. The annihilation was complete. Not a single monument stood indicating that life of any kind survived.

"Any child of ours within the vicinity—"

"Answer our call."

"Who did this to our meal?"

Eventually, in the skies, a roiling black mist assembled. Once it formed into a perfect sphere, it dropped fast as a meteorite. The air screeched in fury and, when it landed, the earth shook and rumbled from the impact.

"Eradication, our second-born—"

"Were these islands—"

"Laid to waste by you?"

"No, Father," she said. "Gormandizer swallowed them long ago, while you yet fasted in your domain."

The anger inside us flared like starbursts, but we managed to hold it down. After all, we could recall our own adolescent days, when the hunger drove us to frenzy. At the end of the Cretaceous, we became that calamity which drove the dinosaurs to extinction, gorging ourself on their scales and meat and bones. No birthling was perfect, and we could weather any such trifling inconveniences.

We surged back to the underground labyrinth, heading for the distant shores of North America. We went quicker now, because our agony had become intolerable. The bloated mass of our body quivered from the sheer want of sustenance. We did not bother searching for our chosen delectables farther in; we surfaced on the borders of the United States, to its closest, most populated city. Los Angeles.

When we broke through the ground, we loomed over what was left of that once great settlement. Like the others, no sign existed that it had ever been more than a concave shell of rock. By then, we would have swallowed a shrub, or even a single flower, had only one existed. But the destruction was absolute.

"Desolation—"

"Are you—"

"The cause of this?" we said, sensing our third-born behind us.

The ocean swelled into a wall of water, stretching up into the heavens. From its midst, buried in the roar of sloshing waves, the expected answer came. "It was Gormandizer."

"Then what is—"

"Left to—"

"Eat?" we snarled.

Desolation trembled, slinking back from the sound of our anger. "Nothing. This planet is a tomb."

The emptiness of our stomach opened new levels of torment the likes of which we'd never felt before. We, who had never loosed our pain as greater than a whisper, now unleashed it in a torrent of shrieks. Rage enveloped us, and we turned to make one last search over the land.

Life may have vanished, but its memory remained in the body of Gormandizer. We'd just have to rip that memory free, piece by piece, and savour its juices upon our tongues. Yes, one way or another, the Feast would commence. And afterward, we would never have to suffer the indiscretions of the first-born again.

ς

We found Gormandizer, a sagging heap upon a flat expanse in the Australian Outback, licking at the dust and clay with his many tongues. When he saw us, he inflated to full capacity, a bulk that matched our own. He had no concern for our anger, never flinched at our approach. Instead, he set his exterior tubular appendages into an agitated twitch, as one suffering an annoyance.

"Father, what business do you have in the world of the living?" he said, his voice full of mockery, his last word slavering from his mouth like regurgitated bolus.

"You have offended us, birthling."

"And it's time you—"

"Paid the penalty."

"Is that so?" said Gormandizer, drawing down his appendages flush with the surface of his skin. "Your children may not agree with your pronouncement."

From below the ground, Desolation and Conflagration emerged. Eradication appeared next, hovering like an uprooted shadow. Already, their bodies were riled into action, their somatic fluctuations hinting at their ill intent.

"Honoured Father, don't do this," said Conflagration.

"Gormandizer acted selfishly, foolishly, but he's still our kin," said Desolation.

"And what you can do to one of us, you may one day do to all of us," said Eradication.

"You only get one warning—"

"My children. Stand with him—"

"And you stand against us."

They did not respond; they only spread themselves around us, one for each cardinal direction.

"I beg forgiveness for what I'm about to do," said Conflagration, attacking first.

With a hesitant lunge, his devouring flames blistered our eastern hide, ripped the moisture from its insides, reducing it to ash. Desolation attacked next, but we quickly encircled him with our western mass. After absorbing his volume through our gonopores, we drew him through our body and expelled him at Conflagration in a concentrated blast. His flames crackled and dimmed, even as the waters of Conflagration hissed and steamed. Soon, both lay dormant, reduced to their most harmless, constituent parts.

Before we could even mend our wounds, Eradication said, "Those two were easy, Father. But none of my brothers can counter aggregated darkness and pure kinetic energy. Can you?"

She billowed, a cloud of black smoke that collected into an orb and rose into the stratosphere. There, she lingered for a moment...and threw herself to the ground. Again, the sonic scream of the descent permeated the air. Her form increased in size at a speed that matched her velocity: at first a grain of sand, a pebble, a boulder, and then an asteroid. We barely had time to gather ourself into a bulbous configuration before she struck.

We felt the full force of her impact. It flattened our centre, pressing our substance to our extremities, pushing our elasticity almost to the breaking point. But only almost. Our centre quickly rebounded, hurling Eradication into the air. She soared farther, farther still, until the far recesses of space snuffed her from our sight.

"One—"

"Birthling—"

"Left."

Gormandizer's body stiffened, taking on a greenish, flustered hue. "Father, we are equally matched, foot by foot, ton for ton. Be reasonable."

"Now—"

"He talks—"

"Of reason?"

"There must be some compromise we can reach. Something that would satisfy your honour and avoid a futile battle."

"Yes."

"Give us life—"

"To eat."

"That's impossible," said Gormandizer.

"Then we—"

"Will feast—"

"On you!"

We propelled ourself at him, an avalanche of squirming, grasping flesh. Gormandizer responded in kind and our bodies met like the collision of tectonic plates. We pressed with all our power, trying to gain ground, trying to prove our surpassing might. For hours we strained, for days we struggled. But as much as it hurt us to admit, the first-born had been correct. He, having consumed so much so recently, and we, wounded and starved, were equals now in every way.

By the end of the seventh day, a notion stirred within the synapses of our central brain. It took only seconds for us to embrace the plan that formed. If Gormandizer could not be overpowered and eaten, perhaps there was another way.

We squeezed our micro-sphincters and gelatinous ooze secreted over the surface of our body—a simple technique we used for folding flesh over wounds. This time we flowed around, not against, the first-born.

"What is this trick?" he said.

"This is no—"

"Trick. We are simply—"

"Healing the breach."

"What are you doing?" he said.

"You wanted to avoid—"

"A useless battle? Well—"

"Here is the solution."

We covered the first-born whole, smothering the cries of fear and panic effusing from his maws. For every inch of us that touched him, our cells intermingled, a fusion of our substances. Then our cells loosened further and his slipped in to fill the empty spaces, expanding our mass, multiplying our innards. Soon, the merging was complete and Gormandizer was no more.

"A fitting—"

"End to—"

"A worthy foe," we said.

And the fourth of us responded, "Agreed."

ς

With the battle won, we burrowed back to our nesting place. There we lay, pondering our fate. Though we would surely wither in the intervening time of slumber, there was enough sustenance within our new body to last for eons to come. The pain would be great and our suffering paramount, but we would endure. Because there was one thing we knew for certain.

Someday, life will emerge and evolve into new and complex forms, the way it has done ever since the beginning. On that blessed day, we will rise from the depths—with empty stomach, quivering flesh, and open mouths—to greet it. And mealtime, that eternal feast, our only enduring pleasure, will commence once more.

Nobody Here
by Bruce Meyer

There is only one way of looking at the world and that way is through a single eye.

To have only one eye is to be beautiful. And when the one eye of your beloved stares into your one open eye, magic happens. That is how we define love. One of the most beautiful moments comes when a soul can look deeply into the centre of another's forehead with a truthfulness and honesty that penetrates to the unity of another brain, a power that is as singular as God.

There was a time, I am told, when to have two eyes was to be beautiful. Authorities used to argue that one-eyed creatures were freaks of nature, monsters that were denied their place in the code of life. To have one eye was to lead a very short and sad life. I read somewhere that one in every 5,000,000 children in the Western Mediterranean came into the world with one eye.

Doctors never held out much hope for such beings. They called the problem *Cyclopia*. They gave us hours to live. Two-eyed parents refused to look at us. They screamed or cried. Some would seize the infant bodies and abandon them so the eye no longer stared back in disbelief that it could not be loved. In the back of their minds, they were frightened that we, of all creatures, had been touched by the gods and were the offspring of unnatural relations.

Much time passed, then the gods returned. That's the legend we own. The gods returned in great illuminations of fire. They took back fire from the two-eyed creatures that had almost destroyed the world.

The two-eyes laid waste to the great lands and left us these islands and their caves and their wild goats. The waves washed over the shores and poured out their tears on every living thing. And when the waters receded and the great lands had turned to black lines on horizons beyond our archipelagos, fish learned to live on dry land with us, and the sunrises became as green as seas and made our flesh, our sea-green skin, the colour of life.

When the great change took place, and the two-eyed gave way to the one-eyed following the storm of all storms, we were outsiders, every one of us. But then we grew more prevalent. We multiplied, one by one. And when our numbers grew large enough we dashed the brains of those with two eyes. How dare they try to give us a second look. We entered their homes as they slept and crushed them the way ancient lore said we could. We invaded the places that the two-eyes thought were sacred. We built ships and journeyed, though we could not tell how far, and arrived in strange lands where fingers of iron poked up from grey stone and spoke of a terrible pain in all things.

And that is when we found *him*, the Crystal Child. He was encased inside a plastic crystal, hovering there between nowhere and nowhere among all the bones and brains and blood vessels in the anatomy lab. They said the place had been called McMaster. And when we found the Crystal Child, the god of McMaster, we fell to our knees, and bowed, and worshipped him. He was eternal, filled with a stillness as blessed as the wind through a meadow of fat, white sheep. His eye stared straight ahead as if he were filled with unity and wisdom and understanding. We looked into his eye as if it were a camera staring back at us, recording our image and reading our thoughts. And when we saw our own reflections in the block of clear plastic crystal that carried him through eternity, we knew we were more beautiful than anyone had ever admitted to us. His single tooth protruded from his upper lip, and a mat of grey-brown hair hovered over the sea-green of his skin. He was the most beautiful sight any of us had ever beheld.

We brought him home to our island and set him up in a cave of his own. His divinity is lit constantly by a small fire, and in the flickering shadows he answers our prayers for love and peace and plenty.

Not long after the great voyage home with our oracle, someone found a book and deciphered what it said. It, too, told the story we wanted to tell of our voyage. But when we read it, we considered it a great abomination. It told, in part, the story of a two-eye who came among us long ago, ate our sheep, drank our wine, and blinded one of our greatest heroes with a pointed stick.

He announced himself as Mr. Nobody.

It was a legend of a warning. He blinded the ancient master, and as the great ancestor screamed in pain "Who are you?" the little two-eyed demon shouted, "I am not Nobody. I am Odysseus." I tried to read further in the book of abomination but I found it a strain on my vision. I simply refused to consider that such evil existed in the world. The greatest evil is to blind one of us. Our eye is sacred because it looks not only outward, but inward. It is the eye into our brains.

When we are born, we are born with a single tooth as well as a single eye. This is significant because right from the start we must sink that tooth into the world and before our hands know how to hold on, before our legs learn how to run, and before our hearts are able to beat with the rhythm of the waves, we must sink that one, powerful tooth into the reality of our island and our history and taste the bitterness of the grapes that have not yet ripened. In other words, we must taste the bitterness of life to know that only our way of seeing is true. That is what we are taught. That is what we live with.

Wisdom is often challenged by accidents of nature. The gods still touch us from time to time in order for us to see the one lone truth by setting it against the perils of duplicity and to show us that we must love that truth because it is singular like we are.

I used to think about this a great deal. I always told myself that if I were tested I would remain true to the one great truth. I would love the one great truth above all else. I swore that I would dash the brains of any two-eye, two-legged creature that came in my way, that I would defend the truth with all my life. That is the pledge each of us makes as we are joined together, man and wife. My wife and I were joined in the sight of the one great truth and we pledged our vision to each other with a unity of purpose.

We would stare into each other's souls for hours, eye to eye, fluttering our eye lashes together the way butterflies permit their wings to touch before they are joined as one. Together, we read each other's gaze as I moved inside her, the way one looks at the stars and sees only one that is truly beautiful among all the others that look down upon us.

After months, the day came when we were to pass that unity to our child. My wife screamed in pain and blood gushed from her belly as our child came into the world. I caught the babe in my hands and raised him up to the light. His arms squirmed and I felt his heart beating, felt the strength of his reach for the ceiling of our cave. I held tight as his legs lashed out and kicked his cries into the stars. And I looked into his face, and my breath stopped.

To my horror, our child was malformed, an abomination. He had two eyes. I turned to grab a club I kept by the door of our home. My wife screamed, asking me what the matter was.

"Two eyes! Two eyes!" I shouted.

She wailed. I raised the weapon above the struggling mass of writhing and bloody little arms and legs as it let out a cry and opened its small, frightful pair of eyes. It knew what I was about to do. The truth had to be upheld. But something stayed my hand. A voice seemed to speak to me out of nowhere, a voice declaring that God was not only one in idea but one in all things and they—my child, my blood, the gift of my loins from the past to the future—were one with me. "I Be, I Be," the voice repeated, burning inside my head as if lightning had struck a tree on the mountaintop.

My wife raised herself on one elbow. "Do it now," she said. "Kill the abomination!" Instead, I cut the cord. I could not crush something that was a part of her and a part of me. The gods had spoken and my heart softened. I sinned. She groaned and cried aloud, "My unity, my unity, why have you abandoned us?" And I wiped the child clean and bathed it in a hollowed stone filled with water and I named him as a father should. I called him Nobody.

Our neighbours heard my wife's screams and mistook her curses for the pain of birth.

"Did she bring the child into the island?" they asked.

And I replied, "Nobody new is here."

And throughout the next several months when they thought they heard a child crying to be fed or to be washed of its sins in the stone bowl, I told them, "You hear Nobody." Over the next several years if I thought they might catch a glimpse of the child, I would distract them by pointing to a bird or a shadow or a rock or a darkness on the waters. "Look upon that, friend," I would say, and they would look away, and the child would pass by silently. My little Nobody grew tall and strong and sturdy as his parents, and when he slept I would stand over him as his eyes closed, and I knew that he could dream more than one dream at a time and that inside his head there were two brains in conversation with each other, one for speaking to the world and the other for speaking to our god.

My wife shunned him but I knew that his vision was more than just sight, that he saw things the way a god sees not just the thing itself, but around it and beyond it. I made him a mask to tie around his head, a piece of goatskin with a single hole punched in the middle of it, so that when he passed the neighbours they would see only one eye upon his head.

I would stand behind a rock and ask him to look at me with one eye. He could not see me. But when he opened his other eye he told me it was as if he could see around the rock. I would hold up several fingers behind the rock when he closed one eye and when he opened two at once he could tell me the exact number.

As he grew older, I took him to the cliff edge to show him how we defend our island by hurling down large stones if our enemies come close. He studied me intensely. His eyes blinked in unison. The next day I found him cutting trees. The day after that, he was lashing the trees together. He made a tripod with a wheel and rope and a rock hanging on a rope from it that could hurl stones farther than any of us. "It is nothing," he said. "It is nothing."

I was awakened from my sleep beneath a large oak tree one morning. My neighbours were screaming, "They are here! They are here! The two-eyes are

upon the wall of the sky and the sea and they are here to kill us or surely to blind us!" I stood up. The Crystal Child had told a neighbour in a dream that this would someday happen, and that if we survived the invasion all the two-eyes would be put to death.

But my son was also asleep beside me with his mask over his face. He stood up, crossed his eyes to peer through the mask's hole, and scanned the wall of the sea and the sky. "No," he said, "they are not here. They are still far away." He pulled off his mask because he said he had to see everything as it was.

"How can you tell that they are not here?" I questioned him.

"Because I can see that they are not here but are growing larger and larger as they move forward for I can see things and tell if they are here or not here, and they are not here. They will be here before noon."

I had taught my son that it was his duty to give his life, if need be, to defend the island from the two-eyes should they ever return. "Father," he had said when I taught him the great wisdom, "my life is in your hands."

We scrambled up the hillside to where nothing stood. Together, Nobody and I loaded stones onto his great nothing, and as the ship full of two-eyes approached nothing made the stones fly through the air as if they were birds. One by one the stones hit the ship and the two-eyes fell into the sea. Some waded ashore and were dashed by the clubs of the neighbours.

"Nobody," I said, "you have saved us with nothing." The neighbours saw how the stones had wings. They saw the great stones drop as if from heaven itself, saw them as if they were a gift from someone high above who made the sky turn black with rage and fury, and they came running up the hillside to greet their saviour. As they approached I realized that Nobody had left his mask under the oak tree, and I could not stop them when they saw he had two eyes. The neighbours fell on him and dashed his head with their clubs.

I cried out in horror to try to stop them. "You are killing Nobody!" I screamed. "Nobody saved you with nothing!"

"Good!" they hollered back and laughed as my son writhed on the ground screaming, "Father, father, why have you let them do this to me?" His limbs twitched as his two brains poured upon the earth and the conversation inside him between the body and the voices of heaven fled to the place where the living dare not go. I sat beside his broken body, the broken body of my son, and wept and wept until I was blind with grief.

When the birds had finally picked his bones clean, and the sun had turned them into the light that glints on the waves when I am near the water, I picked up a tooth of his from the ground and carried it to the Crystal Child as an offering. I stood before the presence of wisdom and unity, empty and trembling. I closed my eye and gave the Crystal Child my son's front tooth. And on top of the Child's crystal, I laid the mask with its one eye poked in the goatskin. There it sat for years, and no one ever noticed it was a new relic among the things we keep holy because everyone assumed it belonged to nobody.

The Imaginary Friend
by Gwynne Garfinkle

1

How it begins: a human girl with brown braids finds me sprawled on my back in the weeds. She stares down at me, and her bespectacled freckle-face bursts into an astonished grin. "Niko? It *is* you! Are you all right?" She helps me to my feet. I'm about a head taller than her.

"I crashed," I say. I remember hurtling towards a green and blue planet, then the impact. It should have killed me. "My space ship…" I look around. There's no wreckage, though there should be. Just a little broken glass and some cigarette butts. How do I know what cigarette butts are? There are no cigarettes on my planet. I'm not wearing my space suit—just a close-fitting corduroy suit the colour of goldenrod (I think inexplicably of a crayon in the girl's small hand) and brown suede boots. The girl has on jeans, sneakers and a t-shirt with a rainbow on it.

"This is the vacant lot, in Van Nuys, on the planet Earth," the girl says. "I'm glad you can breathe our air."

"My planet…" I say, assailed by a terrible memory.

"Exploded," she offers cheerfully. "I know. I'm sorry!" She looks me over. "You don't seem to be wounded. Can you walk?"

I can.

"I'm Gigi," she says. "I'll take care of you, Niko. We're going to be great friends." She takes my hand and leads me past green lawns and one-storey houses with cars parked at the curb and nestled in garages. She sneaks me into her house, into her room.

To my astonishment, there are pictures of me on her bedroom walls. I stare at them. It's me, all right: the same grey fur and amber eyes, the same compact, slender frame in a goldenrod suit. "Where did you get these?" I ask.

She shrugs. "From a magazine."

"How do you know who I am?"

She smiles broadly. "Oh, I've been wanting to meet you for a long time!"

ς

Gigi is ten years old. She manages to keep me a secret from her parents. I sleep in her closet. It's a large enough closet. I don't seem to need food, although I enjoy it when she sneaks me pizza and sandwiches and sweet fizzy drinks.

"I'm so glad you're here, Niko," she says. She says it often. "The kids at school won't talk to me, unless they're making fun of me. I'm not good at sports, and I don't care about the music or TV shows they like. But now I don't care, because you're here. They should be so lucky as to have a friend like you."

"I can't stay forever," I tell her. "I need to build a new spacecraft. Perhaps I can travel back in time before my planet exploded and avert disaster."

She nods. "I'll help you any way I can. With supplies, or anything."

"There are large gaps in my knowledge. I can't remember how to fly a spacecraft, or how to build or repair one."

"Maybe it's amnesia, from the crash," Gigi suggests. "If you want, I can check out some books about astronauts and stuff from the library. But we're not as technologically advanced as you are."

She brings me books about travel to this planet's moon. Nothing jogs my memory. Another thing bothers me: I can speak only the English language, which is odd for someone from another planet.

ς

The movie comes on the television about a month after I arrive, and we sit on the floor and watch it in the living room with the door shut. We even eat popcorn. It gets stuck between my teeth, which are pointed and sharp, but I like it. There is no popcorn on my planet.

I suck in my breath when I see my planet on the television screen—its purple skies and pink-flowered trees.

"But…that's me," I breathe. On the TV screen I wear the same suit of clothes I have on. It's what I wear all the time. It never seems to get dirty.

"It's an actor playing you," Gigi says. "You're the real you. He's Malcolm Pierce. It took hours for them to get all that makeup and stuff on him—plus contact lenses to make his eyes look like yours."

The door swings open. "Mom!" Gigi yells in two descending syllables. "I'm watching the movie!"

"Sorry, honey," says her mother, a small, plump woman with short hair the same colour as Gigi's. I expect her to give a start at the sight of me, but she doesn't even notice I'm there.

"Why didn't your mother see me?" I ask when the door closes again.

Gigi shrugs. "There's a novelization, too. I've read it five times. I'll loan it to you if you want."

A terrible suspicion begins to form—but something on the television screen distracts me. I creep towards the TV. "Aleen," I whisper. It's my wife. She has marmalade fur and bright blue eyes. On the television, she's scribbling into a notebook. Aleen was a renowned philosopher. "Aleen," I implore the TV, as if I can bring her back to life.

"That's Ellen Light," Gigi says. "She has blond hair in real life."

The actress who plays Aleen looks up at the actor who plays me. She pulls my whiskers. "Don't you have anything better to do than look at me?" she teases, smiling. Then there's an explosion outside our home, and she screams.

I brace for the ending of the movie, which surely will be my space flight and the explosion of my planet. To my surprise, the war ends with me still on my planet with my wife. It's the human man and woman (who crash-landed on my planet at the beginning of the movie) who fly back to Earth at the end of the film. For them, and for Aleen and me, a happy ending. How can that be?

That night while Gigi sleeps, I sit in the closet with a flashlight and read the paperback with a picture of me—no, of Malcolm Pierce—on the cover. The book of my life before Gigi. The book too has a happy ending. My suspicions cannot be dismissed.

I open the closet door and sit pondering until the room grows light. Then I steal up to the bed and touch Gigi's shoulder. "I'm not asleep," she says, and opens her eyes.

"Gigi, how did you know my planet exploded? That's not what happened in the film or in the book."

She rubs her eyes and sits up. "How did I *know*?"

"I suppose I should ask, How did you make it happen?"

Her mouth drops open. "I didn't! Not really. I just…I thought about you and the movie. I thought about meeting you. I made up a story about you blasting off from your planet and coming here, and your planet blowing up. I thought it would be so tragic, and I would comfort you."

My head swims. "You thought it would be tragic…"

"I didn't think it would really happen, Niko!" she whispers. "It was just a story I told myself."

For a long moment rage fills me. I press my lips tight together. I shouldn't really have lips, the way humans do—but now I realize that I resemble a human male made cat-like by makeup, foam rubber, and glued-on hair. I let out a great sigh. "It didn't really happen, Gigi. I had no planet. You didn't destroy it, didn't kill my wife. None of it was real, and neither am I. All you did was bring me to life, of a sort."

ς

It isn't much of a life. I come to despise myself for how much I enjoy the girl's company. She made me this way—the perfect friend, visible only to her. It would be cruel if she had done it on purpose. One day we watch an old black-and-white TV program in which a small, all-powerful boy terrorizes his town. Gigi holds my hand tightly while we watch. "It was so *scary*," she says afterwards, eyes shining with delight.

"You're not like that boy, are you?" I ask.

Her lip trembles as if I'd struck her. "You think I'm evil? You think I'd wish anyone into a cornfield?"

"That's not what I meant. I mean, you don't have the power to wish my wife into existence, or to wish me back to my planet. To wish my planet into existence."

"I don't know how! I'm sorry, Niko. I don't know how I did it—I just wished for you, that's all. I wished to meet you, and my wish came true."

"I believe you."

She begins to cry. "I'm sorry if you're unhappy here. Nothing else I've ever wished for has come true. *Ever*."

I place my hand on her small shoulder and pat gently. Her weeping briefly intensifies, then subsides, and she regards me with watery gratitude.

ς

I roam the neighbourhood when Gigi is at school. There's not much to see—squirrels and tricycles, magnolia trees and smoggy blue skies. Occasionally a supercilious Siamese with eyes like Aleen's wanders by. "Hello? Do you see me?" I always ask, but she looks right through me.

One day I try striking out on my own. I walk for an hour along Ventura Boulevard. At a certain point—too far outside the range of Gigi's influence?—I feel myself start to fade. I sink to the pavement. A bus trundles past, exhaust filling my nose. A bicyclist rides right through me. I'm afraid I will cease to exist there and then. I get up and run on all fours towards home.

Time passes, more quickly than I would have thought possible. Gigi turns thirteen.

"What do you want from me?" I ask one day as we lounge on her bed.

"What do you mean? You're my friend."

"But you have a best friend now. It's not like when I first arrived. Why am I still here?"

"I want…" she says. "I can't explain it!" She strokes my wrist, making me purr. I can't help it. She giggles and redoubles her petting. "You have the prettiest, softest fur, Niko."

Sometimes when she's at school, or at her best friend's house, I seem to wink out of existence for minutes, perhaps hours at a time.

2

Posters of sneering musicians have long since replaced the magazine photos of the actor playing me on Gigi's bedroom walls. Some nights Gigi goes to clubs with her friends and comes home with her clothes smelling of cigarettes and her parents yelling at her for breaking curfew. I keep losing time. It seems likely I'll wink out of existence entirely unless I can wrest back her attention. She's infatuated with a twenty-year-old guitarist, skinny and pale and floppy-haired. She spends hours upon hours on the phone with her best friend, analyzing the guitarist's every word and move. "What do you think it *means*?" she asks, lying on her back on the bed. I prowl the narrow room, pacing as her girlfriend's voice on the other end of the line prattles on: *I think Johnny loves you, Gigi! It's so great!*

"He doesn't have beautiful fur like mine," I grumble when she finally gets off the phone.

"What?" she asks, as if she's surprised I'm still here. Why am I still here? She has on jeans and a tight orange New York Dolls t-shirt. She wears contact lenses instead of glasses. Her hair is long and loose. I lie alongside her on the bed. Her parents are out to dinner. I butt my head against her chin and purr insistently. "Hey, your whiskers tickle," she says, giggling, but she wriggles closer. She strokes the side of my face.

Carefully, so as not to hurt her with my teeth, I press my lips to hers. For a moment she is perfectly still. Then she responds with volcanic surprise. "Oh, Niko," she whispers between kisses. "I've always dreamed…"

This, I think, *this* is why I'm still here. I knead her stomach and scratch at her jeans. Her eyes are half-closed, her face flushed. Then she looks at me. "Niko… What about Johnny?"

I growl low in my throat.

"I guess it wouldn't be cheating," she says. "I mean, you're not even real."

I sit up in bed. It's only true. Why then does it hurt?

“Where are you going?” Her arms wind around me. “You are real,” she croons. “You’re real to me.” She pulls me down.

I still long for my wife, though she isn’t real. But neither am I. Just a girl’s plaything. I love Gigi the way some humans love their God, with anger and bargaining and endless yearning. Has she ever loved me, really?

☾

“But Johnny…” She’s weeping on the phone, her eyes red and puffy. Begging him not to leave her. The real one, the unpredictable one, the one who’s visible to the world and not just to her.

She didn’t create him.

“Please, Johnny… I love you… *Please*…”

She hangs up the phone and hurls herself into the pillow. She sobs again and again. I don’t like to see her hurt—but if Johnny has broken things off, it will be just her and me again, and my existence will be safe. I touch her shoulder, and she flinches. “Go away! You can’t help me. I’m nothing without Johnny!”

“That’s not true. You’re…everything.” She doesn’t look up. I don’t think she hears me. I feel lightheaded, unreal. I realize how wrong I was. Heartbreak shrinks her world to a tiny, dense blackness. Her grief is obliterating me. “Please, Gigi…”

“I’m nothing without him. Nothing!” More sobs, blotting me out.

I try to pat her shoulder, but my hand is fading before my eyes. I don’t want to die. “I’m nothing,” I whisper. “Nothing without you.” Then I cease to be.

3

When I come back, it's to a different bedroom. The walls are plain and off-white. I'm sitting on the carpeted floor. Gigi blinks down at me, then smiles. She's wearing glasses again—orange-framed wire-rims—and her freckles have faded. Her hair is cut short. She is a small, plump woman in grey drawstring pants and a purple t-shirt. She pleasantly resembles her mother.

"Niko! It's really you." She gives me her hand and pulls me to my feet.

"It's clearly been a long time since you've spared a thought for me. I should hate you. But you created me to be your willing puppet." Then I see myself—no, that actor Malcolm Pierce—on the TV at the foot of the bed.

"I'm sorry," she says. "I was an idiot. Look, I've been watching your movie on DVD. I hadn't seen it in so long. A new version just came out, and I saw it in the theatre last week. It sucks."

She sounds the same and different.

"Is Malcolm Pierce in the new version?" I ask.

She stops the movie with the remote control and sits on the edge of the bed. "He died a few years ago. No one good is in the new version. It's so slick and full of CGI, but it has no soul. Not like the original."

Somehow I feel flattered. I sit beside her.

"I was a fool to ever forget you," she says. "You were so beautiful. You made me so happy."

She strokes my wrist. I try not to purr, but I do, softly. "I'll stay as long as you like," I say, though I really have no choice in the matter.

She shakes her head. "I figured it out, Niko. It'll be different this time."

"What did you figure out?"

She scoots back until she's sitting against the headboard. She reaches for something on the bed—a small black laptop computer. "How to give you a new story. Because you deserve a fantastic one."

I move up the bed and sit beside her. I peer at the screen—blank whiteness and a blinking cursor.

"Any requests?" Gigi asks. "You should see some of the stuff fans have been dreaming up for you. In this one story I just read—based on the new movie, not the original—you had wild sex with Larren. It was pretty hot."

"With my wife's father?" I splutter, and she laughs.

"I was thinking you could go home, through a time rift, and save your planet. I mean, it was in my version that your planet blew up in the first place, so it seems only fair."

It seems a shame to leave so soon. "I'd like that," I say. "But perhaps first we could brainstorm a bit."

She smiles. "Absolutely! Tell me what you think of this." She begins to type. Her fingers on the keys sound like the falling rain in the pink-flowered forests of my planet.

Skullduggers
by Kate Heartfield

1872

Dr. Vinton sniffed the feverish child.

At the edges of his vision the parents frowned. He had, again, forgotten to disguise his real work, forgotten to open his black bag, to take a pulse or measure the breathing.

He might have been a more successful man, had he stayed in the cities, had he married and paid social calls, had he done the things a respectable doctor should.

As it was, he managed to scrape a living. He was the only doctor for miles, even if he did have a reputation as—what? An eccentric, yes, perhaps a humbug. The world was too bright and busy so he sought solitude and darkness. He had never finished his training but what did it matter, here, miles from anything? They were lucky to have him, these country people, even if they mocked him when he muffled his ears at Yule (too many bells) and when he screamed at the sight of the rope in the country broom-maker's house.

Besides, he had his gift, if one could call it that.

He knew when a patient would live, and when a patient would die, and he could at least contrive to evade responsibility in the latter cases. If this child were marked for death, there would be something under the smell of vomit and old sweat here: the odour he could not escape when his friend George Simmons was alive; the odour he sought now, always, and could catch only fleetingly in the presence of death.

This was how Simmons helped him, still, how he told Vinton what he ought to do next. And Vinton took it as a sign that Simmons must also be the one who somehow helped him evade punishment, all these years. He was watching over him. Somehow Simmons, who could get out of nearly every fix, was keeping the dead at bay.

1855

The room George Simmons shared with Thomas Vinton reeked perpetually of sulfur because Simmons was convinced of the merits of burning out contagion. He stuffed every doorjamb and windowframe with rags. He drew the heavy red curtains across the windows that squinted over Kingston's lazy streets.

Simmons was slight, an American with a past that he kept mysterious. He wore a rakish hat and his word was law among the Canadian medical students at Queen's University.

The last time Simmons burned sulfur in their room, he elbowed Vinton out, into a cool twilight in late spring. Vinton did not bother to ask where they were going. Some of the other students had established a den, just down the road, a set of rooms where an indeterminate number of them slept each night. Simmons and Vinton spent many hours there, in part because their own rooms stank like

Hell's privy, and in part because Simmons liked cards and arguments. There were always more men in the rooms there than there were beds, and sometimes there were women too, especially when one of the boys had come into money.

This night, though, there were only the boys. They played Faro—Simmons' best game.

"Have you got the spade?" asked Burke.

They looked at him, confused for a moment, while he smirked.

"For tomorrow night," Burke supplied, finally, in a tone that implied they were all morons. He made a digging motion with his arms.

Vinton's stomach dropped. "I wasn't supposed to get the spade," he said.

He'd forgotten it. And Simmons hadn't reminded him.

"You were supposed to get the brandy," muttered Simmons, looking up long enough to catch Vinton's eye, before he placed a bet against the eight card.

"No chatter during play," said Bunny, who was the banker, and always worried that someone would cheat.

"I can't believe you haven't got it," Burke said.

"I was supposed to get the *brandy*," Vinton lied, taking Simmons' lead, coppering the eight.

"Granville was supposed to get the spade," Simmons drawled.

Granville was studying, stretched on a yellowed chaise longue. He let his book fall away from his nose and looked toward his friends, his mouth slightly open. Granville was the type to believe that forgetting to get a spade—forgetting even that he had ever been told to get a spade—was something he might do.

"I'll get one tomorrow. How hard can it be to get a spade? Comes to worst I'll buy one."

Burke clapped his hand to his forehead. "No. Tell me you didn't say such a thing. Tell me you never even thought it."

"Blasphemy!" cried Simmons, his eyes flashing. "Traitor!"

Simmons and Burke pushed away from the card table and walked over to Granville, each taking an arm and pulling him to his feet. He rolled his eyes and let them take him.

"Traitors are hanged," said Bunny.

"Hanged it is," said Burke, and he rummaged in a nearby cedar box, coming up eventually with a length of black crepe. "Perfect."

He twisted it, once, twice, thrice, saying deliberately, "We—do not—buy things." Burke knotted it, dancing a few jigging steps, while Simmons held Granville's shoulders with his thin fingers.

"Over the head," said Burke, and slipped the loop over Granville's slight blond head. He threw the end—leaving plenty of slack—over the gas chandelier, which was broken anyway.

Ten minutes later, Simmons slipped the noose off the befuddled Granville's neck, under the pretext of boxing his ears and forcing him to the Faro table, saying, "We need all hands if we're going to stop Bunny from bleeding us dry."

1855

Granville did find a spade, the next day, in the gardener's shed at the university. He walked out of the shed holding it in front of him. That was how the Skullduggers stole, when they stole: proudly and openly, with a sense of entitlement.

So the next evening, with all the equipment ready, the Skullduggers made their final preparations.

The medical school at Queen's University was still young; the university itself had no past and little money. It was, in short, in exactly the same circumstances as its students. That made its students feel as though they had every right to be there—what's more, that the school should be grateful for their presence. The town itself should be holding parades in their honour. Of course the town did no such thing; and so the town, in the opinion of the Skullduggers, deserved what it got.

It was Burke who chose the name *Skullduggers*. He had a gift with words and ideas. He had no gift whatsoever for medicine.

"It is a very delicate matter," young Professor Windlight had said, his hands clasped together, the door to his sitting room closed. He had asked Burke and Vinton there one afternoon after his lecture. Vinton was not sure why he had been asked. He was not clever, like Burke. He supposed people expected him to be a leader, like his father. But he had very little in common with Lieutenant-Colonel Vinton. That was why his father had told him to study medicine.

"A very delicate matter," the professor had said. "Somehow we must supply the table with a cadaver, and yet how are we to do so? The government professes sympathy, and yet it does nothing. It is no wonder medical students have been taking matters into their own hands."

Burke had smiled, watching the professor and waiting. Vinton had tried to look knowing, too.

"It is a curious coincidence, your surname," the professor had said. "Yet I will have no Burkers here, if you take my meaning. You know the stories, of course? Of my countrymen Burke and Hare, and their imitators? Plying victims with laudanum or whiskey and coshing them—it's a blight on our profession. I want no association with such matters, not even the slightest association." He'd shuddered.

"Of course," Burke had answered.

"Yet there have been honest resurrection men," the professor had mused, as though speaking to himself. "Oh yes. Many more of them than most people guess. Men who have managed to extract what they needed without the families being any the wiser. Turf can be replaced, you know. Dirt can be thrown onto a canvas, leaving no trace on the grass. It is all a matter of courtesy, of care, of—"

"Delicacy," Burke had supplied.

The professor had looked at the student, apologetically. "It was your surname made me think of you," he'd whispered.

Vinton had felt sick. He had wished Simmons were there with them; he would have known what to say.

"I'll want compensation," Burke had said.

ς

"Do you really think we should?" Vinton asked Simmons in the darkness.

Simmons shrugged. "I don't see why we shouldn't contribute to our education. We need a body if we're to learn, don't we? It would be pretty lily-livered to expect other fellows to do the resurrecting."

He had a way of putting things. Vinton went to sleep, his conscience clear.

ς

Granville happened to eavesdrop on a conversation in Hurdman's general store, so he heard about the death first. He didn't do anything about it, beyond telling Simmons.

Among Simmons' many gifts was the ability to ingratiate himself with anybody's relatives, especially relatives who were female and over forty. The Skullduggers had only ever heard him discuss four subjects: a) cards b) the human body c) Voltaire d) germs. Put him at a picnic with a mother who gardened, though, and Simmons could talk for forty-five minutes about the best traps for slugs. Or let him lean against a fireplace near an aunt who was the leader of her local temperance organization, and Simmons was full of anecdotes of young men who had met their ruins at the bottoms of bottles.

So the first thing Simmons did, as soon as he heard of the death of old Bridie Cavanaugh, was to leave his card with the grieving family. The Cavanaughs had never heard of him, of course. But Simmons was so stubbornly and immovably overcome with grief at the Cavanaughs' door that the servant who took his card was quite at a loss.

And the kindly female cousin who had stationed herself in the hall between the drawing room and the morning room heard everything and bustled to the servant's rescue, because it didn't do to have a distraught young man on the doorstep, whoever he was. And so the cousin began speaking with George Simmons, a student of divinity and a great friend and admirer of Mrs. Cavanaugh, who would of course be honoured to come to the wake, and who humbly offered his services, and those of a friend, to watch over the body the first night after it was put in the ground.

ς

"To the Skullduggers' first adventure," said Burke, raising his glass.

They drained their glasses and looked around, somewhat ill at ease.

"Granville and Bunny, you're on lookout. One at each gate of the graveyard."

"What's the signal?" Simmons asked.

"What signal?" Granville asked. "Nobody mentioned a signal, did they?"

"If someone comes, what are you going to say?" Vinton put in, pleased with himself that he had caught Simmons' meaning. "You can't very well shout, *Someone's coming so stop robbing that grave.*"

"Vinton, we aren't robbing graves," Burke chided. "In fact, let there be no confusion on that point. We take no rings or earrings, nothing but the body. It's not property so it's not theft. Only mischief. The worst it will net us is a fine."

"Which is as good as jail, because none of us can pay it," grumbled Bunny.

"Oh, shut up, Bunny," Burke said. "Simmons and Vinton have a point. What are you going to do? Can either of you do birdcalls or anything?"

"I don't think birds call in graveyards at night," said Simmons. "Besides, I can't imagine one could slip a birdcall into a casual conversation. At night. In a graveyard. They should just call out to us, in a natural way."

"Who?"

"Bunny and Granville," said Vinton, catching Simmons' eye, catching on. "Imagine a busybody asks Bunny what his business is. He says, *Just out for a walk. Trying to shake the cobwebs clear. We've been up all night studying. But then my friend wandered off—to look at a grave.* Yes, *To look at a grave. Hey! Granville!* See, you shout that last part. Then if we hear someone shout *Granville!* or *Bunny!* we'll know there's trouble."

"Admirable, Vinton," said Simmons. "Just one thing. In case anyone does suspect something, probably best not to use their real names, eh?"

"Right," said Burke. "Smith. That's the only name we use."

"Smith it is," Granville said.

"The night's not getting any longer," Simmons said. "If it were done, when 'tis done, and all that."

"We're not stabbing anybody," Burke said.

ς

It was a chilly night for early June. The three diggers had all brought gloves, as much for warmth as for work, but Simmons' were the longest and thickest. He hated to get dirty. Still, he took his turn with the spade with morbid determination, while Burke and Vinton rested and smoked. It was Simmons who struck the coffin.

"My God, it's shallow," Vinton said. "You'd think they'd made it easy for us on purpose."

"Maybe they did," Simmons said, leaning on the spade. "No point in prolonging the inevitable when there's a medical school nearby. Nobody likes a mess."

They brushed the dirt away from the top, the light from the lantern skimming along the coffin's edge.

"Do we pull the whole thing up, or open it?" Vinton asked.

"Open it," Burke said. "Much easier."

They stood silently for a moment. Then Burke said, "We're going to have to open it eventually anyway. We can't pull a coffin through the streets on that—" and he gestured at the wagon they'd brought. "We have to bundle it up, make it look nondescript."

"And what exactly are people supposed to think we're pulling? A bundle of blankets, through the streets, at one o'clock in the morning? One way or another, if someone sees us, we're caught," Vinton said.

"If it's a bundle that looks suspicious, well, that gives people the chance to put their faith in humanity's goodness and trust that all is well, despite their better judgment. But if it's a coffin, out in plain sight, well, that doesn't leave much room for the benefit of the doubt, now, does it?"

"Let's just do it," Simmons said, and vaulted lightly down on top of the coffin. "Are there catches or anything? Locks? No, wait—it looks like it's smooth all the way around. A door that wasn't made to open. Nailed shut, though, I suppose. All right, help me up. Let's get that crowbar."

Opening the coffin proved to be the most difficult labour of the night, and the most wracking to their nerves, because it was noisy work. Every time the wood creaked apart, or the crowbar slipped and hit the wood, they paused for a moment, still as frightened frogs in the grass. But no one came.

They pulled the old woman out, wrinkling their noses, although the faint smell was indistinguishable from the damp smell of the living clay of the grave.

They filled the grave and carefully replaced the sod. Simmons wrapped the corpse in two sheets, and then they wrapped it in a Hudson's Bay Company blanket, and then they folded a quilt and put that on top.

"Get on," Burke said to Simmons.

"What?" Simmons asked.

"Come on. This is the only way to disguise it. You're drunk, and we're pulling you home from a party."

"You get on."

"You're the smallest, Simmons."

"Oh, give it up, Burke," Vinton said. "I'll do it." Vinton put a hand gingerly on the quilt, and found, to his relief, that he could feel no distinguishable body part underneath it.

"You're too heavy," Burke said. "It has to be Simmons."

"I'm already on. Now go." Vinton lifted his leg up and sat, his knees folded up and his arms wrapped around his knees.

"Lie down," Burke said. "You're supposed to be drunk."

"If we see someone, I'll lie down. Now go."

They pulled the laden wagon, with some difficulty, along the graveyard path. They could see the gate shadowed against a flickering streetlight, and the silhouette of Granville leaning against it, smoke rising from his pipe. He straightened up as they approached. He called something, but they couldn't make it out.

"Shut up, Granville," Burke hissed. "We'll be there in a minute."

Granville ambled toward them. The three diggers saw another silhouette approaching, behind Granville. It was a man, holding a lantern.

Granville shouted, "Smith! Smith!"

"God, what a fool," Burke said. "All right, boys. Time to lay it on thick."

"Oh, Jesus," Simmons said. "It's her brother."

"It's whose brother?"

"Her brother," Simmons said. "The body's brother. I met him at the wake. What the hell is he doing here? Wait, hold up. Any closer and he'll recognize me. I'm supposed to be watching the grave, for God's sake."

Mr. Cavanaugh made no sign of recognizing Simmons, but he did seem to understand that he had happened on a grave robbery. (It might have been the spade that Burke was carrying because it kept slipping off the wagon.) But instead of confronting them, Mr. Cavanaugh turned and ran away into the street.

Granville ran to the group and said, breathlessly, "Do you think he knew?"

"Of course he knew," Simmons said. "He's gone to get help. We've got to get out of here, now."

Granville cringed.

Simmons said, "Vinton, hit me."

They gaped at him.

"Listen. Here's the story: I was watching the grave with Granville. He got spooked and I said he could go wait for me by the gate. I was by myself at the grave, when a gang of resurrection men came by. They hit me, and as I was lying there unconscious they did their dirty work and left. Granville saw it all and started to get help, when he saw the obscured form of Mr. Cavanaugh and mistook him for a man he knew. One Mr. Smith."

"Well, I can't think of anything better," Burke said.

"Of course not," Simmons said. "Vinton, now's your chance for revenge on a horrible lodger. Give me a good one, right in the face."

Vinton shook his head. "I'm not going to—"

Burke said, "Granville, you do it."

And Granville, for once in his life, did better than he or anyone else expected. He punched Simmons, hard, and when his fist came away Simmons had blood on his eyebrow.

"Christ!" Vinton whispered.

"All right, let's go," Burke said.

Simmons really was reeling, but he waved them on.

"I'm staying," Vinton said.

"That doesn't fit the story," Granville said.

"Go," Simmons wheezed. "Straight to our place, Vinton. That's where they'll look for you."

"Best if the group splits up, anyway," said Burke. "Look smart, lads."

Vinton ran with the others to the far gate, while Simmons stumbled to the grave of Bridie Cavanaugh, his hand to his head. Vinton stopped at the gate, looking back, and saw Simmons sinking to the ground to wait for his accusers.

Vinton listened to Burke hiss at him, and to the rumble of Granville's worrying.

"Go on then," he whispered, harshly, still frowning into the distance where Simmons lay huddled on the ground. "Go on."

The others ran off behind him.

Vinton strode to a tree and hid behind it. Any minute now, Cavanaugh's brother would be back, with police perhaps, or a friend. Any minute now Simmons would act the part of the guard of good faith who had scared off a gang of resurrectionists and been punched hard for his trouble.

Vinton hid, his gloves to the bark, leaning into it and watching around its edge. He watched as mist became rain, greying the world. The rain fell on the quilt that covered the body of Bridie Cavanaugh, abandoned on the wagon in the middle of the cemetery.

He watched until the sky turned pale, and horses and carts rolled through the streets. Still Simmons lay still and black as a shadow, and there was no sign of that man—the brother of the body. Vinton was shivering so badly now that he felt that his muscles would never be still again.

"To hell with it," he said, his words hanging heavy in the chill air. He left his tree and walked, as quickly as he could without risking the indignity of running, to where Simmons lay.

ς

He walked Simmons through the streets, holding him by the upper arm. Simmons was acting very much like a man who had had too much to drink—not as he, Simmons, would act after a few whiskeys, not sardonic, impudent and bleak, but like a lesser man would act: incoherent and staggering. Vinton walked him, forcibly, up the stairs to their room. He threw open the door and they both coughed from the sudden blast of volcano-rot.

"Your damned fumigation," said Vinton, through a dry throat and red tears. He lay Simmons down on his bed and rushed to the window, covering his mouth and nose with one glove. He yanked the window open and covered up the sulfur. He rushed back to Simmons, who lay mumbling on the bed.

"If I had been the one to hit you, as you wanted, I wouldn't have hit you as hard as that clod Granville did."

Simmons shook his head. "It wasn't being hit that made me ill."

"If I hadn't let you lie in the cold so long—"

"Hush!" Simmons said, and started to cough. "Listen."

Vinton hushed.

"Forfeit," Simmons said. "All of us. Forfeit. The dead—they will take all of us."

Vinton was still sitting by Simmons' bedside when two men came to the open door.

"He's dead," he croaked, looking up at Mr. Cavanaugh and the policeman. "Simmons is dead. Granville hit him. I didn't think—I didn't realize."

"We have Ronald Granville already, and the rest of your gang. Come along then. It seems it's murder been done tonight as well as the desecration of an old woman's grave. A fine bunch they're raising at the university," said the policeman.

Vinton heard very little of it. There was a ringing in his ears and the smell of sulfur in his nose and he was, he felt sure, forfeit. He had wronged the dead and the dead would not forget it.

"What do I do?" he asked, weakly.

"You come with us," the policeman said.

ς

Bunny and Burke died of a fever in jail. Ronald Granville hanged for the murder of George Simmons in the autumn of 1855.

By then, Vinton was on the stagecoach for Ottawa, his family having paid the fine. He was the only one left alive. The only one not yet forfeit.

Vinton knew death would catch him soon: perhaps tomorrow. As the years stretched on, the world of the living became less and less tolerable; it seemed designed to remind him of his cowardice, his dishonour. Too bright. Too noisy. It set him on edge and he never seemed to know what to do next.

He pretended sometimes that Simmons was with him, guiding him, giving him advice. That he had come with him to the back of beyond, as his assistant. Sometimes Dr. Vinton set up a chessboard or a game of cards and played both sides, imagining what Simmons would do.

Tomorrow, or the next day, he would smell brimstone and he would be with Simmons again. He waited.

1872

Dr. Vinton bent by the little girl's mouth and listened to the rough breath, as if he might hear a whisper in it. He breathed in, three times, but detected no odour of brimstone. Finally he sighed and stood up.

"The child will live," he said.

The mother put her hand to her mouth. "Then why do you weep, doctor?" she asked.

Vinton put his hand to his wet cheek. He wept because the child would live, damn her. He wept because he had hoped to catch a breath from that world, the world where he ought to be.

His life was forfeit after all. This was his punishment, this waiting.

"What should we do?"

He blinked. The child would live. He had a standard reply in these circumstances.

"Broth and good air," he said thickly. "Send for me tomorrow if the fever does not break. If I am not in, my assistant, Mr. Simmons, will come."

The mother looked at the father.

"We have never met this Mr. Simmons," she said. "He was not there the last time, with Jenny, when you said—"

His stomach dropped. He had forgotten again.

"Of course," Dr. Vinton said, gruffly. "Mr. Simmons is often called away, as I am."

Still he did not know how to answer the call.

The Escape
by Nicole Cushing

Homely, awkward, too-tall Candace said that when she ventured outdoors she felt caught between the thumb and index finger of a giant, invisible hand. "Whenever I'm outside, I feel the pressure of a disgusted world trying to squeeze me out," she said. She said she felt like a zit on the face of the world—a zit that must be burst to make the world more beautiful. That, she explained, was why she'd been admitted to the hospital at which I was a psychiatrist.

I was, of course, dismayed by her lack of self-esteem, but also pleasantly surprised by her skill at shaping a metaphor to convey her subjective experience of agoraphobia and depression. Most patients aren't that silver-tongued. I told her I was impressed.

"But it's *not a metaphor*," she said, through clenched snaggle-teeth. "I'm talking about real pain, dammit! It started years ago as a tickling sensation, something grazing against my skin. But it keeps getting worse and worse. Graze became touch, touch became grip, grip became squeeze, squeeze became crush! The pinch gets harder, more vise-like, each time I go outside. It's already gotten to the point it's unbearable. And, some day soon, it'll get so bad that I'll pop. If I go outside again, I'll be reduced to shreds of fallen pimple-skin and the clear pus inside me will fall on the grass like dew. Put yourself in my shoes, Doctor. Can you imagine how it feels to be so hated by the world that it tries to eliminate you? To have to hide indoors from the hand? To have to worry about what will happen when the hand figures out a way to enter buildings? Can't you understand, now, why I feel so hopeless? Don't you know I'd do *anything* to end the torture?"

My heart sank. Maybe this sounds awful, but I was *hoping* she was depressed and agoraphobic (rather than paranoid and delusional). When patients are depressed, they can engage with you in meaningful conversation with some therapeutic benefit. You can tell them it's always darkest before the dawn, and it seems to help. When patients are anxious, you can reassure them that their fears can be overcome, with enough hard work. Anxiety patients and depressives engage a psychiatrist's bedside manner and psychotherapy skills. Delusional patients, on the other hand, tend to reduce a psychiatrist to the role of PEZ-dispenser-for-pills. Talking to such a patient is like talking to a toddler.

Why hadn't I checked Candace's admitting paperwork beforehand? A brief review of the police report would have saved a lot of trouble. It confirmed that she was utterly insane, too far gone to benefit from talk therapy.

She'd been living in a scuzzy apartment in the south end. The building had been condemned, found unfit for human habitation. There were no working toilets, and hadn't been for months. The roof leaked and had been left unrepaired. The foundation had begun to buckle. And yet, when authorities attempted to arrange the safe evacuation of the building she refused to vacate the premises. She told the cops the giant, invisible hand would squeeze her again, and she couldn't guarantee that this time it wouldn't pinch her so hard she would burst.

She denied having any friends or family she could move in with. Quite naturally, the officers brought her here. Their report indicates she wriggled and cried when escorted out of the house, as though she were being crushed. They noted even worse theatrics as she was being escorted from the squad car to the hospital entrance.

I completed her assessment and treatment plan. I prescribed her Zyprexa to make the giant, invisible hand go away. I also recommended the slow introduction of recreational therapy, focused on gradually exposing her to the outdoors. I felt justified in making that recommendation. It only made sense. The antipsychotic medication would make the giant invisible hand go away, and the recreational therapy would *convince* her the giant invisible hand *had* gone away. The two would work in concert.

I was at a luncheon sponsored by a pharmaceutical company on the day she escaped. It was an overcast, ugly day outside. It had rained for much of the night before, and a heavy wind still gusted. I was surprised to learn they'd even taken *the patients out*. But the incident report written by the orderlies says that many of our charges were particularly wound up, that day. Not so much Candace, but the rest of them. Like rowdy elementary schoolchildren, they needed to blow off steam. They needed recess. So recreational therapy was held outdoors, in the area we call "the meadow" (actually, just a grassy soccer field).

The orderlies' report indicates that Candace seemed a bit out of it when they led her outside along with the rest of the patients. Oddly, she didn't protest going outdoors. She went willingly. Maybe that's because the medicine was working and the delusion was starting to lose its grip. Maybe she was too disoriented and sedated to even *know she was going* outside. Or maybe she *planned* to escape.

In any event, she was last seen lingering next to the ten-foot-tall fence at the edge of the meadow, looking into the dense grove of trees on the adjacent property. She showed no signs of trying to climb out. She was just standing there. Some of the patients say they saw her start to wriggle and cry. The orderlies can't confirm this. They had to take their eyes off of her and focus on two toothless, elderly schizophrenics who'd gotten into a shouting and shoving match. They only realized something was amiss with her when they heard a loud pop—like the uncorking of a champagne bottle—come from the space where she'd been standing.

The incident report states that when the orderlies heard the noise and jogged over to see what was the matter, they found nothing but "shreds of a huge, soggy pink water balloon" where Candace had been standing. The final report on her escape deduced that local hoodlums must have come over to tease our patients, found her there by the fence, and tossed that water balloon at her. Then, she must have become enraged and found her way over the fence to get revenge.

Our security teams searched the wooded area on the other side of the fence, but found no trace of her. Television reports of the escape yielded no tips.

For several days afterwards, the hospital administration banned patients from the meadow, citing security risks. But eventually they relented and allowed the more stable patients outside. Since the day of the escape, the weather has taken a surprising turn for the better. It would be cruel, indeed, to deny the patients the right to experience one of the more beautiful weeks anyone can remember.

Death, in Three Acts
by Sara Puls

Act One: Exteroception

Nika does not like knowing the exact moment she will die. She does not like knowing by whose hands, whose command, whose shiny torture tools her end-fate will come. Most of all, she cannot stand being trapped inside this wheeled deathbox, bound to her seat by Enri's hands, by his bone-thick chains, by so much impossible pain.

"Just a precaution," Enri says sadly as he settles into place beside her. He will stick with her until the end. Like a loyal puppy, like a fool.

"For your own safety," her brother Yohav adds as he climbs into the driver's seat. Then he turns around and looks at her with watchful-owl eyes. He will get her to where she needs to go, of that Nika is sure.

Without another word, Yohav turns the key, puts the vehicle into gear, and pulls it onto the street. Enri tries to force a smile but Nika looks away, scoffs, then calls them both *idiot-pricks*. They should not have come. They aren't making this any easier. They could get sick.

She calls them idiot-pricks again, this time with a modifier: *fucking. Fucking idiot-pricks*. She has always liked the way that word has tasted, the way it has rolled off her tongue. She wants to say it as much as possible now, while she can. While there's time.

She says those words a third time, relishing the way they clang against the metal walls of her travelling prison cell.

When Enri and Yohav don't react, she fights for their attention by thrashing and kicking, the ring-ting of the chains burning in her ears as she moves. In the back of her mind, she knows her actions are like some kind of horrible foreshadowing of what's to come. She knows that what's voluntary now, won't be in the end.

She has seen how the virus works.

When Nika stops thrashing, Enri tells her not to worry. He uses his finely groomed, well-tuned, nice-doctor voice. He tells her that the change will be relatively painless. That her brain won't really perceive it, that it won't really hurt.

She doesn't believe him. Because no one knows for sure. Because by that point in the transition, not a single victim has managed to speak a single goddam word.

And because her shoulder—her wound—hurts like bloody hell.

As Enri's words fade into the ether, Nika turns to look at him. He is still wearing his scrubs. She tries to guess how many times he's had to say those words since the outbreak. *Don't worry. It won't hurt.* She shudders, looks away. She must have said them a thousand times herself. In just a matter of days.

Enri puts a hand on her shoulder and whispers into her ear, "Just look outside, baby, and try to enjoy the ride."

Because everyone knows Nika bought a discount ticket for a one-way trip. Everyone knows what awaits her at the end of this quest.

She sighs and forces a thin smile, then looks out the windows on the stripped-down ambulance's double doors. She looks and watches everything pass. The streets are jammed bumper-to-bumper with cars. The still-healthy are trying to escape, to make their way to the suburbs, the farms, the tiny Midwest towns. Undoubtedly some of them only *think* they're healthy. Some of them are already sick.

The virus will spread.

Because that is what viruses do. Viruses spread and clocks tick. Tick, tock, tick.

She cannot bear it. She looks away from the busy streets, tries to ignore the taxis' buh-beep-beep impatience and the little girls' tear-stained eyes.

To be forced to perceive the outside world, to sample and savour it, to touch and taste it, to bite it off and chew, chew, chew it like thick cud, all the while pretending to be seduced—it is too much. Christ, it is too damn much. Nika doesn't have it in her. Not even crocodile tears can she wring from her eyes.

Yes, anyone who pretends to enjoy their last bit of life once their end-time is slated is a lying *bitch*. That's what Nika knows. She didn't know this before. But she does now. Because…

…Because she is acutely aware of every bump and curve of the street, every whistle of wind outside, every lace of smoke emanating from the cigarette stub pinched between Yohav's fat-sausage fingers. And yet it is impossible, *fucking impossible*, to enjoy any of it.

Because if this is going to happen, it should be simple. A nice clean period. Punto. Finito. End.

Because fuck semi-colons, fuck exclamation points, and absolutely *fuck* ellipses, those dread-filled lingering sons-of-pricks.

Because if Enri is right, if she's actually sick, then in three hours and thirty-seven minutes, she will be dead. That's how long the virus-magic takes to complete its act. Four short hours.

Virulent whore.

If only she knew *how* she would finally expire. If only she understood the virus better. Maybe she could enjoy her last minutes then, resign herself to her fate.

She looks down at her wrist, burdened by chains. But she can still see it—still make out the face of her watch.

Three hours and thirty-two minutes.

At least she has the watch. It's a small speck of good fortune, a cookie-crumb bit of luck, in an otherwise total-shit hand. Her mother gave her this watch, gold-faced with a slim band, for her sixteenth birthday. They had been fighting over cake—stupid, meaningless cake—in the kitchen. Finally, tensions too high for anything else, both Nika and her mother broke out laughing. They laughed till they cried, then hugged and hugged. The tears not yet dry, Nika's mother took the watch from her wrist and looped it gently around Nika's. As she clasped it tight, she said, "Savour every moment, Annika. Always remember what's important. Before it's too late."

Nika had nodded, tight-lipped but so, so happy. She'd been eyeing that watch since before she could talk, entranced by the shine of its face in the light, the way it complemented her mother's gold skin and honey-brown hair.

Three hours and twenty-four minutes and the memory of her mother is too much to bear. She needs something else to take its place, to fill her zombie head.

She clears her throat. "Where are we going?" she asks, her words cutting through the silence like an axe through ice. The ambulance-turned-hearse has very little working for it in the way of acoustics. It makes all sounds seem ominous, harsh, cold.

In the front seat, Yohav says nothing. His face is frogskin slick. He's nervous. And yet he isn't wearing a mask. Neither is Enri. They must figure a thin swath of fabric won't keep them from catching this beast. They must figure that if the virus wants them to catch it, they will.

Nika knows this thought should affect her, should make her stomach twist-clench with dread. But it doesn't. Because she won't be around to see it happen, to see them get sick, to see the whole world turn to shit.

"*I said*," she snaps, "where are we going? Where are you guys taking me?"

Yohav hunches over the steering wheel, narrows his eyes, and pretends not to hear.

How nice. My own brother already can't bear to look me in the eye.

Just a short time ago he was insisting he had to come, had to be there for his little sister, to protect her till the end. Maybe it's dawned on him that he didn't protect her then, that he can't do anything now.

Nika turns to Enri, who swallows, sighs, and runs a shaky hand over his scalp. His right leg starts to bounce—up-down, up-down—jackhammer quick. His lower lip quivers. He is nervous. Anxious. On the verge of tears. Enri has never been those things.

"You know where we're taking you, Nika," he finally says. "Please"—his voice cracks, oozing thick-hot pain—"please don't make this any harder than it already is."

And then, through the cold chains that bind her, Enri squeezes two of Nika's clammy fingers with his. Because she does know. They're taking her to a hole in the ground where they'll drive a screwdriver or bone saw or some other shiny-sharp object into her skull. They'll wait until the last minute, until they're absolutely black-ice clear it has to be done. But they'll do it. They aren't cowards. And then they'll toss her in the hole and bury her like road-kill, like a rabid dog.

Because the sick do not get better and they do not go home. They go…they go… Okay, so Nika doesn't know *exactly* where the sick go. Outside of the city, that's for sure. Beyond the river and watershed, obviously. But more than that… she can't say. She hasn't concerned herself with it—until now.

And what does it matter, the precise location of her death-hole?

She should consider herself lucky. The dead without connections—without doctors for boyfriends and nurses for brothers, without hospital administrators for bosses—they get burned in piles, flung in crisp-crispy heaps into mass graves. She's an exception. She gets a personal escort. She gets time to reflect. She gets her own private hole in the earth.

Whatever that's worth…

Just one day ago, she was not sick. She was reading poetry and drinking tea, carrying on. She did not have these red-hazed eyes, these jerk-twitch muscle ticks. Just one day ago, at the start of her emergency room graveyard shift, she was fine.

A puff of morbid laughter on her lips, she goes back to staring out the front window. To trying to ignore Yohav's head, bald but for a few wisps. They're siblings, but so different. He is big and wide and olive-skinned. She is short and thin and ice-milk white. He always wanted to work in the medical field. If not for their father, she would have been an English teacher or a journalist. Yohav is alive, Nika is almost dead.

Everything outside is dead. Strangled or subdued by winter's raw grasp. This surprises Nika. For some reason, whenever she pictured the end times, the apocalypse, she imagined summer. Hot weather, green-green trees, sweat dripping from the brows and backs of the sick and the unsick alike.

She closes her eyes. Something niggles at her brain, like a toothpick at sore gums.

There were so many people with the signs last night. So many people trudging through the doors, then leaving on wheels with white sheets draped over their prostrate bodies, that she forgot to check the guy's pulse. And then, one second later, it was too late. His teeth were tearing into her flesh, sampling a sticky charcuterie of Nika-muscle, before she had a chance to move, to cry, to run.

How could I have been so stupid? The thought rang-tangs against her skull like a bullet, like warm and heavy droplets of molten metal rain. *So goddamn dumb.*

But Nika knows why. Nika has always been an apostrophe. Taking shortcuts and cutting others out, pushing things down. She isn't elegant or careful, not when compared to Enri or even Yohav. She lives in a perpetual spin-twirl hurry, taking the quickest, fastest route.

Without warning, tears burst from her eyes like water from a failing dam. The liquid blurs her vision, blocking out Yohav's shape, the windshield, the world. She feels the wet stick of tears on her legs, the thin, green-blue fabric of her scrubs clinging to her skin like a bad dream. Her head falls forward, aching, just aching, to be held by her hands. But of course her hands are cuffed and bound. If she needs comfort now, she will have to take it from Enri.

Fucking lucky bastard, Enri.

The timing of that thought is impeccable. Because now his hand is on her shoulder again, his deep-smooth voice like rain pattering rocks in her ear. "I love you," he says. "I will always love you."

Nika looks at Enri and immediately wishes she hadn't. His eyes are filled with water, two black ponds. Ponds so deep that if she leans in, stares deeper, she'll drown.

"I love you, too," she chokes out. "And I'm sorry." Earlier, she hadn't responded to his tender words. She'd been too worked up. She is only slightly calmer now, but her desire to see him suffer has faded.

She just wants this to end.

Three hours and two minutes.

Enri puts his warm-with-life lips to her ear. "It wasn't your fault," he whispers. He has regained some of his composure, wiped the tears from his cheeks. "And I'll never, ever forget you. My beautiful little carrot."

Nika cringes and shakes her head. *No, no, no.* She doesn't want to hear his words, his voice, his silly-sweet nicknames. She's been his *little carrot* since she tried to dye her hair blond for some fancy medical association gathering three years back. The colour came out bright orange instead. It was right before Halloween, though, and Enri, with his usual calm, collected brilliance, decided they'd both dress up in costumes so no one would have to know. Nika went as a carrot. Enri donned all green and went as carrot-tops. At the end of the night, he called her the most beautiful carrot in the world.

She *is* his carrot. But she isn't complete without him. Nor he without her.

And nothing in the whole world is fair.

As they enter the tunnels that lead away from the city, the deathbox becomes a dark-damp solitude, lit only by the ash-flickering glow of Yohav's cigarette and by the white of Enri's forced smile.

Nika closes her eyes, tries to focus on what she loves about the world.

In sleep's sticky-fingered grasp, Nika dreams. She dreams of ice cream cones and clowns at the fairgrounds. She dreams of shimmer-glimmery parties in the hospital atrium, and how they inevitably spill out, into the street, down to the corner bar. She dreams of the dim sum at her favourite restaurant in Chinatown. And then her dreams twist and choke, cough up dark blood in her brain. A nightmare emerges from the blood, painted onto the inside of her skull in red smudges, like a disturbed child's finger-paint game. Her eyes are sewn shut with barbed wire, her wound cauterized with acid that smells like lilacs and piss. The words to her favourite poem crawl off the bloody page and force their way into her mouth, blocking her airways, filling her lungs. Her heart is ripped from her chest and replaced with an ice chip. She chokes, she dies, she rots.

Eventually, Nika wakes. She wakes and immediately wonders what it will feel like to have a stake driven through her brain. *Will it feel like a sinus infection? Will my skull make a snap-pop sound like a bursting balloon?* The thought snuck up on her, climbed out of some little black hole in the side of her head, and now sits just behind her eyes, putting razor-fingered pressure on her nerves and discolouring her view of the deathbox, of Yohav and Enri, of the skeleton-bare trees whizzing by outside. She wants to take Yohav's cigarette (his third? fourth? fifth?—she's lost track) from his fingers and burn the horrendous thought from her mind.

She leans forward a bit, eyeing that ash-glow-flicker and then looks away just as Enri's fingers, soft and warm, meet her chin, pull her face to his.

Seeing him—his almost-black eyes—her mouth opens like a knife-wound gash and she laughs. The sound is made of glass, shattering against the walls, the floor.

"Relax," he coos.

But she can't. Biting back the tear-sting joy of his touch, Nika spits on his shoes. Snarls. Spits again.

Then she jerks back, with a clipped gasp, shocked. She didn't mean to do that; she hadn't planned to do that. Any of it. The action was...involuntary.

Enri knows this too.

Without a word, he finds her fingers through the chains, but it's no use. Inside her now is something new. She can feel it in the impossibly deep furrow of her brow, the bone-crushing clench of her fists. She is a firework, a red-rage hurt, tick tock ticking as the fuse begins to burn.

And then there's a needle-stick, a Nika-subduing serum trick. *Morphine?* She can't quite tell. *Maybe it's some other sleep-inducing cocktail. That's good,* she thinks, *I could really use a stiff drink right about now.*

"I'm sorry," Enri says. "But it's time. Just breathe. Just relax." She eyes his lips, which are dark and round, slightly puckered. Ready for a kiss.

It hadn't crossed Nika's mind that she wouldn't be *her* enough to see where they take her, that she wouldn't last long enough to see her hole in the ground.

Enri kisses her forehead and she knows that lip-skin touch will be the last thing she ever senses, really senses, of the outside world.

Act Two: Proprioception

Intermission ends. Nika regains some sense of herself. And this next scene starts with a feeling. A feeling that there is something lodged in her ribcage, pushing her lungs painfully far apart from one another. She thinks the something is snakes. Yes snakes, writhing and twisting, curling around each bone like poisonous ribbons, hiss-hissing into cruel question-mark shapes. Definitely snakes.

And in her brain, too. In her brain there are bite-sized flies, putting pressure on her optic nerves, blinding her. Her eyes are open, that much she can sense, but the world is dark.

So. Damn. Dark.

And in this sort of darkness, time is meaningless. She is in that middle place between dead and undead. Maybe. It is damn hard to tell.

It is all a question mark.

Earlier, she'd forgotten about question marks. She does not want a question-mark end. A question mark—pure, complete not-knowing—would be worst of all.

Her body is prostrate now—perhaps lying on the bench in the ambulance, perhaps not—and a bit difficult to move. She cranes her neck, sense-searching

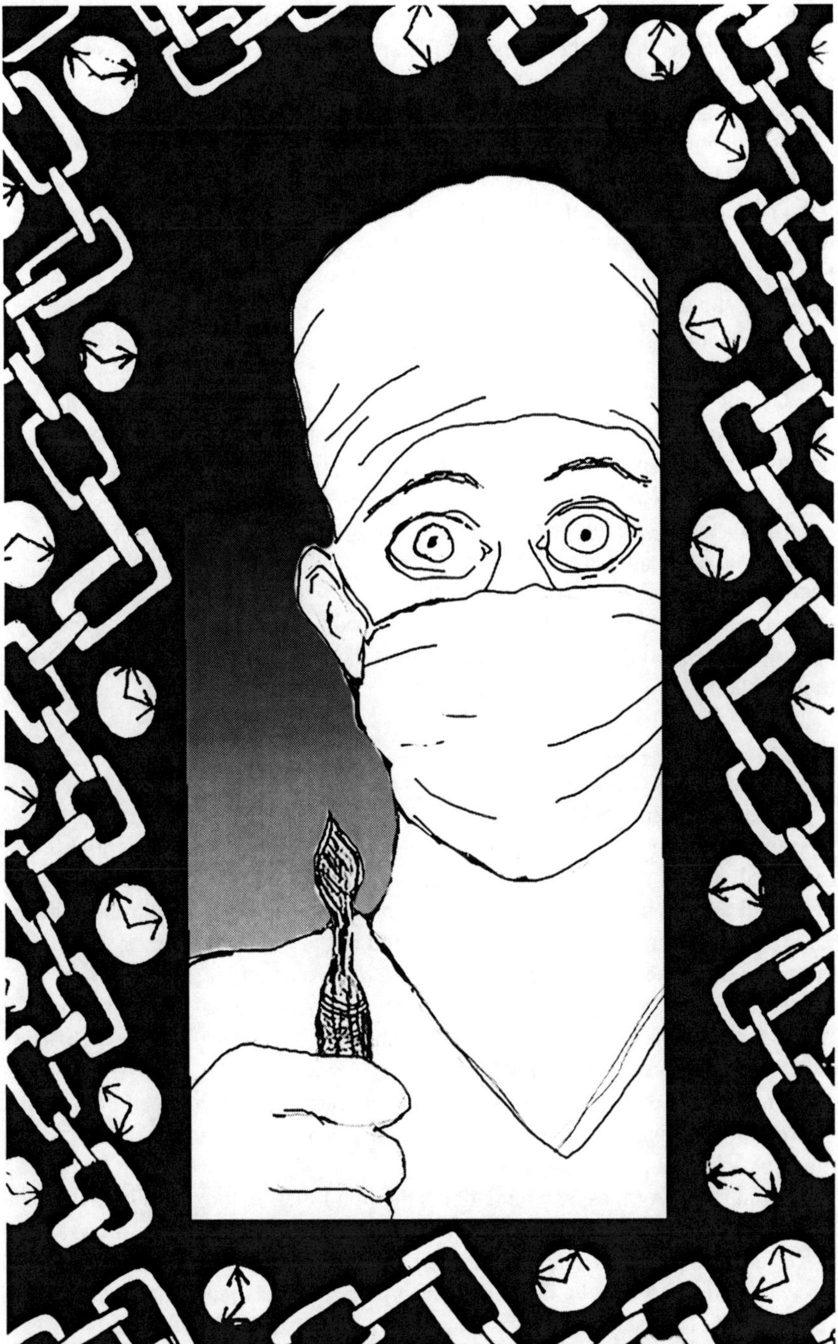

for Enri or Yohav even though she cannot see. The movement hurts—there is a sludge-thickness in her neck muscles, in her blood. And she cannot sense them, cannot even hear.

She waits, longing for the period. The end of the sentence. To be done.

But like the gymnast who knows her body well enough to turn it five-hundred-forty degrees, head over hands, on a four-inch-wide balance beam, Nika can sense this isn't it. Not quite. Her body, though stiff and summer-sun hot, is still hers, still responding to her commands. She can tell how far apart her feet sit from one another, she can feel her knees trembling, she knows her wounded shoulder is swollen and throbbing.

She wonders what it looks like—her shoulder. *Necrotizing Fasciitis? Gaping boils? Something worse?*

Unable to do much but wonder, she closes her eyes and lets tears fill the space between her eyelids and eyeballs, hot and soothing like tea. Just as she begins to smile, a needle-toothed pinch takes her by surprise, biting into the back of her skull like a nail pounding through wet, rotted wood.

Nika tries to scream, to beg them—someone, anyone—to stop the circus carousel of virus-spun agony. She opens her lips and takes a breath, readying herself to push the words out in little puffs of sticky anger. *Help, help, somebody fucking help me!* She huff-puffs, but no sound comes out. Her throat collapses in on itself, rocketing down into her stomach like a rollercoaster veering off its tracks, plummeting to a crash-bang death.

Act Three: Interoception

Everything is dark and quiet. Darker and more quiet than before. And Nika is alone, inside herself. *Move, leg,* she thinks. *Lift, arm.* But she cannot move or even cry. She hears no huff-puffing, no grunt-scraping of limbs fighting to remain alive. No, they are gone now. They belong to someone—something—else. And there is no world. There are no words. She is that much closer to death.

Her mind wanders. She thinks about God or the gods or whatever's out there, waiting. She tries to imagine oblivion, tries to decide if she can sense Something More. She wonders if she'd even deserve *More*, assuming it exists. But it's too late. Too little and too late. All she can do is wait.

Minutes left. Seconds, perhaps.

And there is this horrible ache, a hell-heat creeping up inside her, boiling the marrow in her bones. It began inside her toes. Deep inside, deeper than she knew the depths of toes to go.

Thinking about toes, she remembers the first time she took Enri to the Adirondacks, to her parents' red hut-of-a-cabin with only a wood-burning stove for heat. Enri was a city boy through and through, but he loved the place anyway. *I can't believe the stars!* he kept saying. *I never knew they could be so bright.* Yes, the stars. They are what she loved most, too. Thousands of little asterisks painted on the black canvas of night, reminding you of what's important. Reminding you to savour it while there's time.

Oh god how she wishes she and Enri were there now, dipping their toes in the ice-cold November water, daring each other to jump in, tasting the freezing air on their lips, relishing the chill in their bones. Because Nika never did learn to savour a moment, not really. She was always on to the next thing, fitting in more, more, more. Even if it meant her work was sloppy, her hobbies were performed with half-hearted enthusiasm, her lover was only almost-pleased.

If she could do it all again, she wouldn't be such an apostrophe. She would know everything is important, every letter of every word.

When Nika wrests what remains of her brain from this memory-pain, the hell-heat has filled her stomach with fire. It rages, melting her from the inside, like rabid hunger. Solid flesh turns to liquid—she feels every plip-drip as it drops and splatters against her bones. And her bones turns to liquid calcium that flows like thick, hot cream, filling the space in her head.

No one is really ready to die. Not in the end. Especially not like this. She wants to fight it. Oh yes, she wants to fight. God how good it would feel to win. She wants an ellipsis or a semi-colon or even a fucking question mark. Because not knowing, not feeling the end—or knowing it's still far, far in the distance—seems so much better than this.

Seems like bliss.

But there it is: an image of Enri's dark, puckered lips. Like a small dot. A tiny black period in her mind. And Nika knows what this means.

As everything else melts away, she finds it in her to move her lips towards his. And the kiss of death is quick, like a needle prick, like a single keyboard click. Like a graceful final bow.

The Poetry

Sandra Kasturi, introduced by Dominik Parisien

Greetings, *Postscripts to Darkness* readers. In this third feature we look at Sandra Kasturi, Canadian poet, writer, and co-publisher of Chizine Publications. She has won the prestigious Arc Poetry Magazine Poem of the Year Contest, and her poems and stories have appeared in numerous venues, including *ON SPEC*, *Prairie Fire*, *Shadows & Tall Trees*, and the *Chilling Tales*, *Evolve*, and *Tesseracts* anthology series.

Kasturi is a poet of transformation, and it should come as no surprise that her collections *The Animal Bridegroom* and *Come Late to the Love of Birds* are full to bursting with creatures. Changelings, wolves, mermaids, bees, serpents, and, of course, all manner of birds. In her books, a burning woman fits in a canning jar, poets are birds of prey, you can pluck and eat a planet, and Daedalus twists the truth of a plump Icarus's death. Kasturi knows the masks we wear, and the beasts and the birds that lie beneath, and her poems contain the cruel lessons of the darkest fairy tales, tempered by charm and wit.

For this feature I have chosen three poems: "The Secret History of the Human Body," "Venice Letting Go," and "Moth & Memory." All three are prime examples of Kasturi's exploration of change, of the things that are no longer what they seemed and that, in certain cases, what they never were to begin with. More strange and wonderful transformations will appear in her next poetry book, *Snake Handling for Beginners*. Kasturi is also working on a novel, *Medusa Gorgon, Lady Detective.*

The Secret History of the Human Body

"The body is our first haunted house. We live in it. We haunt it.
We are literally our own ghosts."
—Michael Rowe, author of *Wild Fell*

What if you are the cuckoo in your own nest.
The haunter of your own body.

You feather yourself with diadems
and strange moonstones.

Things that reflect, tether you
to this odd house, this flesh architecture.

You open the door of your mouth
and creep out on the doorstep of your tongue.

Scurry back down your own throat,
linger like a cold fricative.

The flickering lamps of your eyes
go on and off without intervention.

That knocking in your head, your own hollow steps
from frontal lobe to medulla oblongata.

You disappear from your body
if anyone looks too closely.

Cultivate the stories, the sparse mythology
of empty premises, fingers that move by themselves.

You become that strange presence felt by others.
The icy spot in the room your own breastbone.

Late at night, you take your own hand
in the darkness. Deny that it is you.

Venice Letting Go

It was like Venice letting go of the pretense of being attached to land.
—from "The Vervain" by David Keyes,
I Do So Worry for All Those Lost at Sea

Let go of the carnival,
dark dear heart,
the old familiar masques
and marauders, the dredged
canals of the mooniest
reflected moon. Let go
the bilge pumps
and the gaudy gondolas.
Raise each finger gently
from the edges of land
and float away, Venice—
drift toward the great-finned
open sea, with its sawtoothed
mermaids and its saltlick
heart. Drift away
from the resolutions of soil,
the firmness of tree roots
and terraces. Slip away
from your sinking. Comb
through the tangled limbs
of kraken and cuttlefish.
Drink from mollusc shells
and send telephone messages
by conch or albatross. Toss
your knives and forks overboard
and use only tridents for eating.
Let go of your attachments,
Venice, dear Venice. Leave
behind the rigours of fences
and borders. Take your ancient
palazzos and antique linens,
your dusty wine bottles
and red glass goblets
and say a final farewell
to land. Become
the iridescent bubble dream
on the wavecap, the pop
of gilded fairytale foam
you were always meant to be.

Moth & Memory

for Michael Rowe

Plume moths remove remembering.
Their feathery snowtouch on the eyelids
sifts out thought and will,
leavens facts until they rise
into the air and pop
into oblivion.

Moths' delicate footprints
on the skin, invisible
as sorrows, chase away
longing and desire, chase
knowledge of things.
Of self, of trees and acorns,
glass jars, death and daisies,
gazelles and geodes.

All of it, gone.

Until we are blank, unfurrowed,
smoothed right out of our lives,
scooped out like a hollowed melon.
Moths whirling around our heads,
a petal-storm of white hawthorn,
each flick of wing counting
back, removing month, day, minute,
unravelling selves and selvages.

Knowledge of moths, too,
goes in the end. The final thing
to slip away; the last
touch we feel: moths'
shivery tickle on our bodies
become meaningless.

Say goodbye now, before moth
and memory give way to air.
Say, farewell Death's Head, fare-
well Emperor, Luna, Elephant Hawk.
Polyphemus. Io. Mottled Beauty.
Memory, goodbye. Plume moth
mottled memory, goodbye.

The Contributors

M. Belvin is a freelance illustrator and roller derby player based in Ottawa, Ontario.

Carrion House aka Luke Spooner lives and works in the South of England. Having graduated from the University of Portsmouth with a first-class degree, he is now a full-time illustrator and writer for just about any project that piques his interest. Despite regular forays into children's books and fairy tales, for which he has won awards for literary and artistic merit, his true love lies in anything macabre, melancholy, or dark in nature and essence. He believes that the job of putting someone else's words into a visual form, to accompany and support their text, is a massive responsibility as well as being something he truly treasures.

A passionate artist and illustrator, **Alyssa Cooper** has always been fascinated by the darker side of fiction. Born and raised in Belleville, Ontario, she works freelance as a graphic designer whenever she's not busy writing books of her own. Alyssa is currently living in Kingston with her cats and a personal library.

Nicole Cushing is an author of dark fiction. Her debut novel *Mr. Suicide* will be released by Word Horde in July 2015. She is the author of the novellas *Children of No One* (nominated for the 2013 Shirley Jackson Award) and *I Am the New God*. She lives in Indiana.

Lisa de Nikolits is the author of *The Hungry Mirror* (2011 IPPY Awards Gold Medal Women's Issues Fiction; long-listed for a ReLit Award) and *West of Wawa* (2012 IPPY Silver Medal Winner Popular Fiction; *Chatelaine* Editor's Pick). A *Glittering Chaos* tied to win the 2014 Silver IPPY Popular Fiction. Her fourth novel, *The Witchdoctor's Bones*, launched in spring 2014 to literary acclaim. *Between the Cracks She Fell* will be published in fall 2015. These are all from Inanna Publications.

Joel G.'s art can be seen on safety posters, album covers, portrait restorations, tattoos, Ex Libris stickers, *Postscripts to Darkness*, *Lackington's*, and a weird colouring book called *Postcards from the Spacefarm*. He lives in Ottawa with his partner, Renée, their cats Dee Dee and Amadeus, and a cabinet full of cat medications.

Gwynne Garfinkle lives in Los Angeles. Her fiction and poetry have appeared in such publications as *Strange Horizons*, *Interfictions*, *Mythic Delirium*, *Apex*, *The Cascadia Subduction Zone*, *Shimmer*, and *Goblin Fruit*. She is working on a couple of novels, as well as a book of poems inspired by classic films, TV, and pop culture.

James Greatrex is a multi-media artist and filmmaker. He is also known for blacking out after binge drinking single-malt whiskeys, mean-spirited and confrontational observational humour, and being an all-around downer at social gatherings. Follow his bi-yearly posts on Twitter @dayzchain4satan and his "experimental" (read: unpopular) film uploads on YouTube @ sodarkfilms101.

Kate Heartfield is a fiction writer in Ottawa, Canada. Her work has appeared in *Strange Horizons*, *Crossed Genres*, *Lackington's,* and *Daily Science Fiction*. Her mythpunk story "Six Aspects of Cath Baduma" appeared in *Postscripts to Darkness 4*. She is a member of Codex, SFWA, and the East Block Irregulars. By day, she's the opinion editor of the *Ottawa Citizen*. She is working on a historical fantasy novel.

Alis Kellar is an illustrator and digital artist based in Ottawa. By day she works as a graphic designer, by night she draws weird things and makes noise in the electro-industrial band Encephalon. Creating both traditional and digital artwork, she is usually inspired by the surreal, macabre, and mysterious.

Sandra Kasturi is a poet, writer, and editor and the co-publisher of the World Fantasy Award-nominated and British Fantasy Award-winning press, ChiZine Publications. She is also the co-founder (with Helen Marshall) of the Toronto SpecFic Colloquium and the national Chiaroscuro Reading Series. Sandra's work has appeared in various venues, including *ON SPEC*, *Prairie Fire*, several *Tesseracts* anthologies, *Evolve*, *Chilling Tales*, *A Verdant Green*, *TransVersions*, *ARC Magazine*, *Taddle Creek*, *Abyss & Apex*, *80*! *Memories & Reflections on Ursula K. Le Guin*, and *Stamps, Vamps & Tramps*. Her two poetry collections are *The Animal Bridegroom* (with an intro by Neil Gaiman) and *Come Late to the Love of Birds*. She is currently working on two books: *Snake Handling for Beginners*, and her first novel, *Medusa Gorgon, Lady Detective*. In the past, Sandra has been a blackjack dealer, a fake TV psychic, and a professional calligrapher. One of those is true.

Mariel Kelly lives in Toronto where she mostly draws comics about everyday life. She spends a lot of time with her big black cat and, although she mostly enjoys the cute things in life, she is always happy to tell you about her nightmares.

Tonya Liburd shares a birthday with Simeon Daniel and Ray Bradbury, which may tell you a little something about her; and while she has an enviable collection of vintage dust bunnies to her credit, her passions are music (someday!) and, of course, words. One day she hopes, when introducing herself as a writer, that she won't feel all weird about it. She's hard at work completing her novel. She is also the Associate Editor of *Abyss & Apex Magazine*. This is her first published story.

MANDEM is the art name shared by Maize Arendsee (an art instructor and Studio Art MFA student at Florida State University) and her life-partner,

Moco Steinman-Arendsee. Drawing on an academic background in classical mythology, gender studies, and critical theory, MANDEM works across media and materials, intentionally destabilizing genre. MANDEM has received numerous art awards, including Juror's Merit at the LaGrange National XXVII and First Place at the Museum of Fine Arts (Tallahassee, FL) 2014 Summer Annual. While being widely published and nationally exhibited, MANDEM remains actively involved in the Tallahassee art scene.

Samuel Marzioli was born and raised and that's all you need to know about that. His work has appeared or is forthcoming in numerous publications, including *Apex Magazine*, *Intergalactic Medicine Show*, *Shock Totem*, and *Penumbra eMag*.

Bruce Meyer is author of over 45 books including the forthcoming collection of short fiction, *A Chronicle of Magpies*, and the recent poetry volumes *The Seasons* and *Testing the Elements*. He lives in Barrie and is a professor at Georgian College and the Victoria College at the University of Toronto.

Christine Miscione's work has appeared in various Canadian publications, such as *Exile: The Literary Quarterly*, *This Magazine*, and *The Puritan*. In 2011, she was the recipient of the Hamilton Arts Award for Best Emerging Writer. In 2012, Miscione's story, *Skin Just*, won first place in the Gloria Vanderbilt/Exile Editions CVC Short Fiction Contest (emerging writer category). Her debut short story collection, *Auxiliary Skins*, was released through Exile Editions in 2013. Her first novel, *Carafola*, was published by Mansfield Press in late 2014.

Silvia Moreno-Garcia's debut novel, *Signal to Noise*, about music, magic, and Mexico City, will be released in 2015. Her first collection, *This Strange Way of Dying*, was a finalist for the Sunburst Award for Excellence in Canadian Literature of the Fantastic. Her stories have also been collected in *Love & Other Poisons*.

Sara Puls spends most of her time lawyering, researching, writing, and editing. Her dreams frequently involve strange mash-ups of typography, fairy creatures, courtrooms, and blood. Sara's stories have been published in *Daily Science Fiction*, *The Future Fire*, *GigaNotoSaurus*, *Penumbra*, World Weaver Press's *Fae* anthology, and elsewhere. She also co-edits *Scigentasy*, a gender- and identity-focused spec fic zine. On Twitter, she is @sarapuls.

Before turning to speculative fiction, **Robin Riopelle** was a professional adoption reunion intermediary, a museum curator, and a children's book illustrator. Her love of historic houses and contemporary fringe cultures comes together with supernatural elements in her fiction. Her debut novel, *Deadroads*, was published by Night Shade Books in April 2014. A transplanted west-coaster, Riopelle lives in Ottawa with an absent-minded professor, some adorable children, and far too many pets.

Alexandra Seidel dabbles in the alchemy of words. The results are less metallic, more inky: you can read them at places like *Lackington's*, *Mythic Delirium*, *Strange Horizons*, and others. If so inclined, you can follow Alexa on Twitter (@Alexa_Seidel).

In certain Oakland neighbourhoods, dusk shadows can be collected with a silver bowl. If kept in a basement at a consistent chill, the shadows congeal into a thick soup. Pour into mud through a sieve fashioned from pages of old books. Leave overnight. By morning a hopeless, insomniac writer will bloom in a bed of strange flowers. **Arley Sorg** is a strange Oakland flower. A 2014 Odyssey workshop grad, he works at *Locus Magazine* and writes.

Gregory St. John is an artist and fiction writer living in Gainesville, Florida. If he is not painting or sculpting, tending to his gardens and chickens, studying history and science, reading while walking his four dogs, cooking, or building something, he's hard at work at the family perfume business, Solstice Scents. He is currently drafting his first novel and editing a collection of his short stories entitled *The Short and Curlies*, featuring: "The Presence of Hell," "Servant of Stone," "A Helping Hand," and "The Dare."

Rob Thompson's hobbies include eating expired medication and dancing spastically, half naked, to video game soundtracks. Currently, there is a sizeable reward for his capture, either dead or heavily sedated.

Tomasz Wieja is an illustrator, photographer, and art director based in Poland. A graduate of Fotoacademie Rotterdam, he combines studio and location photography with photomanipulation in order to seek out new undiscovered realities. His work has been exhibited in galleries in the Netherlands and Poland, printed in the prestigious GUPNew Yearbook, and nominated for the Dutch Photo Academy Award. He currently makes up part of the Treslettres Collective.